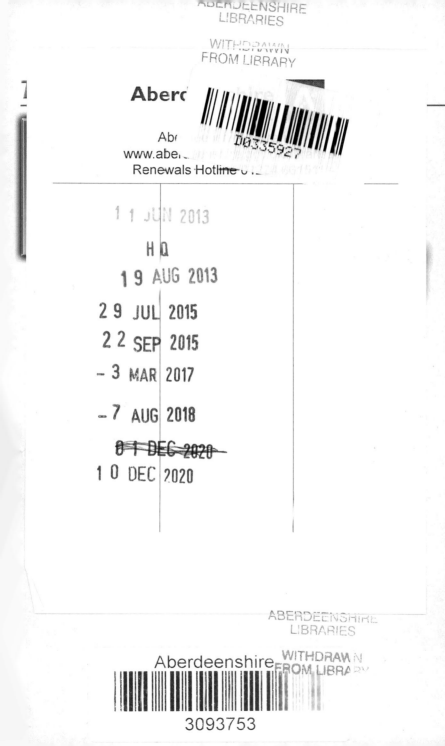

Time Traveller

Paul Morris

Seven Arches
Publishing

Published in 2012
By Seven Arches Publishing
27, Church Street, Nassington, Peterborough PE8 61QG
www.sevenarchespublishing.co.uk

A catalogue record for this book is available from the British Library.

Cover design, scans and typesetting by Alan McGlynn.

Printed in Great Britain.

ISBN 978-0-9567572-6-5

To Judy
TIBI MAGNO CVM AMOR

‹IF THIS IS THE FIRST TIME YOU HAVE READ ONE OF THE BOOKS THAT RECORDS THE ADVENTURES OF CHILDREN FROM THE TWENTY FIRST CENTURY IN A TIMEZONE DIFFERENT TO TODAY. YOU NEED TO KNOW›

> That SHARP stands for The Scientific History and Art Reclamation Programme.

> That STRAP stands for the Scientific Testing and Recording of Aggression Programme.

> That time slip is something that you might suffer if you travel through time and space, in a similar way to how some people get jet lag when they fly long distances on a jet air line.

> That if you travel through time and space you are a xrosmonaut. If you are an experienced xrosmonaut you are entitled to put Xr after your name to show your rank.

CHAPTER 1

Downtime

Diamond-bright, sharp and hard as a crystal, the light shrank to a single point. It spun slowly, pulsing blue-white as the space around it dimmed to black. From far off, from the very furthest edges of hearing, there was a faint, high-pitched whine, a piercing note of shrill sound coming nearer and nearer until it filled the whole room then... Nothing.

The screen went blank and the deadly words appeared: GAME OVER.

'Better luck next time, Danny!' came a voice from the doorway.

Danny Higgins spun his chair round, the game controller poised in his hand, a momentary scowl of frustration frozen on his lips. Bad enough losing just when he thought he was in front, but maddening that his younger sister witnessed his defeat.

Seeing his black scowl, Jenny dropped her cheery grin. 'Oops, my bad,' she mumbled. Sticking on her 'concerned sister' face she asked, 'How far did you get this time?'

'Last level,' grumped Danny. 'Flipping, flipping middle of the last flipping level!' He grabbed two handfuls of his hair and growled softly. Jenny's look of lip-chewing sorrow made Danny burst out in a spluttering laugh.

'Oh, it's not that bad. I'll survive. Just about.'

'Good,' Jenny chirped, her grin popping back into place, 'cos your lunch is ready. Mum sent me to get you.'

'Be right down,' said Danny.

'Wicked. And Dan...'

'What?'

'Don't give up your day job!'

Jenny ducked out of the door, narrowly avoiding the screwed-up ball of paper Danny flung at her.

As her footsteps fled along the landing and faded down the stairs, Danny padded across the room and picked up the crumpled paper missile. He teased it open, flattening it roughly on his desk, and read over the neatly-printed, short lists of words he had written there. They were the names of school subjects mostly, grouped into the categories – arts, languages, technology and the humanities. He read them over for the umpteenth time that day, still no nearer to making a decision.

But he would have to decide, and quite soon. At nearly fourteen, his Year 9 options could not be avoided – the difficult choice of the subjects he could choose to study in Years 10 and 11:subjects that might shape his life for the next goodness-knew-how-many years. GCSEs. A-levels. College. University. The rest of his life. It was already the June mid-term holidays, and next week he would be back at school for the last few weeks of Year 9.

Fighting off the rising urge to freak out, Danny scanned the crumpled page. It was a huge decision, and he had looked all over the place for help. The government's advice website told him sunnily to think about what sort of person he was, what he was good at, what he enjoyed doing, and take it from there. So he had added another list to the page, noting that he was (he thought) a calm, methodical, thoughtful person; that he was careful and caring; and that he was almost obsessively tidy. In another list he noted that he was (he thought) friendly and sympathetic – a 'people person'; that he was observant, sharp-minded and that he was good at swimming and running.

Then it all came unstuck because the last list – what he enjoyed doing – would have to include something he could never write down: what he really enjoyed more than anything else was travelling through time. If he was going to tell the whole truth, he would have to write that he was actually a time-travelling secret agent for SHARP, an organisation from earth's far-distant future; that for two years he had roamed through time for SHARP, gathering information about what was, for them, the world's long-lost history, the history lost in the mysterious disaster they called the Dark Chaos; that he had already carried out several successful missions and a daring rescue.

He was not the only one. He knew that SHARP had at least one other operative, a young girl and he suspected there were others though he had never had contact with any of them. He knew, too, that there were agents who worked for a rival organisation, the rogue outfit STRAP, the dark force that threatened the peace and stability of the future world – and perhaps the present one. Danny had met two of their agents – he had had to rescue one of them – and he was sure the recruits did not know what they were getting mixed up in. STRAP put their kids in danger and didn't do anything to protect them. SHARP had put Danny in contact with the two recruits and he had patiently tried to explain their situation, tried hard to persuade them never to work for STRAP again. Yet would they? STRAP could be persuasive, cunning and dangerous.

But was it all so simple? SHARP and STRAP, good and bad, heroes and villains? There were things that had happened to him that made him wonder whether he really knew the full story...

'Hello again!' Jenny's far-too-cheery voice, shot at the back of his head from a range of two metres, made Danny jump out of his skin. He clutched his pounding heart, his cheeks burning with adrenaline.

'Sorry, did I nearly kill you?' Jenny's grin was cute but devilish.

'Phew! I was miles away. Didn't hear you coming.'

'It's my ninja training!' She cleared her throat. 'Ahem. Message from Mum: *Daniel Simon Higgins, stop whatever you're doing and get down here for your lunch right now or you'll find your delicious, extra-seedy ham salad sandwich inside next door's dog.* End of message. Thank you for listening.'

Danny closed his eyes with a sigh. When he opened them Jenny had vanished. For a ten-year-old she would make a good ninja, flitting about silently, half-killing people with shock. He flicked his computer monitor off and hurried downstairs. All this stuff about SHARP and STRAP would just have to wait.

Two things cheered Danny up when he arrived in the kitchen. The first was the delicious smell of the fresh, nutty bread his mum had brought back from the baker's. The second thing was the music drifting from the smart little flat-panelled music player, one of the few really modern gadgets his parents owned. Both keen historians, Danny believed they would have been much happier living in some long-past age before newfangled stuff like electricity, cars and zips were invented.

The machine was only a few days old. If you stuck your nose up to it, it smelled of fresh plastic and newness but the music it was playing was far from new. It was one of the Baroque music CDs the family had brought back from their long weekend in Venice. Though they rarely took holidays, Mr and Mrs Higgins had decided that a special treat was in order. They had been saving up for two long years to have a new extension built onto their house, scraping together every spare penny and insisting on what they called 'staycations'. That meant holidays at home, getting to know their own country rather than flying off overseas. Then, incredibly, the family had drawn a winning lottery ticket. *Five thousand pounds*! It had been enough to pay for the extension *and* a decent holiday – always assuming, as Dad said, that they didn't stay anywhere too posh. So they had jetted off to Venice for three glorious days in a two-star hotel by a little canal.

Venice was full of canals; it seemed to be built straight out of the blue water of the Adriatic Sea. At first unsure whether he would like the place, Danny had discovered that he loved every minute of it. Every morning he had woken to the sound of the local gondoliers on the canal outside, rowing their long, sleek black boats, singing songs and shouting at each other in furious Italian.

They had explored the narrow streets, bought colourful carnival masks, ridden on the *vaporetto* bus-boats and visited an endless stream of art galleries and museums.

'Vivaldi?' asked Danny, addressing nobody in particular.

Jenny paused mid-chew, and stared at him as though her brother had suddenly started speaking Martian.

Rachel Higgins looking up from her book and extra-healthy sandwich, pushed her glasses up her nose and focused on Danny, who had already sat down at the table and started on his sandwich.

'Oh, the music? That's right, dear, it's by Antonio Vivaldi.' She looked quizzically at her son, as though he was some strange creature she had found strolling through her salad. 'Baroque music, Danny?' she queried. 'I thought you liked all this modern bleep-and-squeak stuff.'

'Mmm, I do,' Danny replied between bites, 'but I like this too. It's soothing. Good for the brain.'

'And the digestion,' mumbled Jenny, starting to chew again.

They munched on for a few moments in friendly silence.

'Isn't this Davide playing the cello?' said Danny.

Caught mid-bite, Sandra Higgins went slightly red. Danny and Jenny exchanged glances. Every evening in Venice the family had been to a live music concert. They had accidentally discovered *Interpreti Veneziani*, the best musicians, their mum said, in Venice. The group played at a beautiful old church, San Vidal, and they were incredible! Rachel Higgins had bought a handful of their CDs. And everyone had agreed that she had had a bit of a crush on the brilliant cellist, Davide Amadio, especially after she had stayed behind to get his autograph!

Danny had wished he could ask SHARP to send

him back to see what the ancient city was like hundreds of years ago, when Venice was a world superpower. Perhaps he should ask Kazaresh, his contact at SHARP. If SHARP ever contacted him again that is. If Kaz ever replied to any of his texts. If they ever...

'You didn't hear a word I just said, did you?' asked his mum. 'I said, have you got any further with your decision?'

Danny looked blankly at his mother.

'Your Year 9 options?' explained the patient Mrs Higgins.

'Sorry, Mum. Err, no, not really. But I'm getting there. Well, sort of.'

Mrs Higgins put on her best 'concerned parent' expressions. 'Have you talked to Mark and Griff? It might help you to straighten things out to talk things over with friends.'

'Mark's been in Florida, Mum, and Griff's at a Centre Parc somewhere. But don't worry, I'll sort it before school starts back.'

'You won't make any final decision without agreeing it with Dad and me, will you?'

'No, of course, not.' Swallowing the last bite of sandwich, Danny bolted for the privacy of his own room.

CHAPTER 2

Off The Day They Did Social Skills

Danny flipped the 'no entry' sign that dangled on the outside door handle, closed the door and threw himself full-length on his bed. He stared at the ceiling for a few minutes, fingers laced behind his head, humming quietly.

Then he got up and tidied his desk, aligning the edges of his computer monitor with those of the work surface and placing the mouse neatly in the centre of its mat. He lined up the edges of the books on his shelves – they were already laser-straight – then picked up some bits of fluff from his dark carpet. When he found himself standing at his window, counting the gnomes in the garden opposite for the umpteenth time (there were more than ever – were they breeding?!), it was no good: Danny had to admit it. He was *itchy*. Not that fingernails-on-skin, scratch-your-head sort of itchy. This itch was right inside his head, right in the middle of his brain. It was the only way he could describe it to himself: an itch. A vague, pointless, niggling irritation right in the centre of his mind.

He tried to pin it down. It had started a few weeks ago. Now it was driving him nuts. An uneasy feeling, like there was something right in front of him that he was missing. Like he was the only person in the room who didn't understand something, when everyone else did.

Maybe it had something to do with school, the headache of getting his Year 9 options figured out. But how hard could that be? Just choose the subjects he really liked, or was best at, and he would be halfway there.

No: school was part of it, but it wasn't the whole story. If only his mates had been around. Or maybe if he could speak to Kazaresh. Kaz was his contact at SHARP and Danny had come to think of him as a friend, but Danny had not heard from Kaz in ages. Months.

Danny was a good agent: he had realised that in the two years he had worked for SHARP. Kaz had said he was one of SHARP's best, maybe *the* best. He had travelled to distant centuries, rescued people, seen things no twenty-first century boy ever would. He had been told by Professor Aurelia Dobbs, Kaz's tutor, that by working for SHARP he would be helping to prevent the ultimate destruction of the world. That when he or any other agent went back into the past, SHARP would be able to detect the traces of evil, cruel actions that left something called fracs behind that would somehow let in evil to spread destruction throughout history like the seeds of a horrible weed. He had totally bought into that and still did. It had made everything seem okay – the danger, the secrecy, the having to lie to his family. But now, because he hadn't heard from SHARP for such a long time, somehow doubt was creeping in. When had that started? Was it after he had found out about the other organisation, the so-called rogue outfit STRAP? Yeah, that seemed to be it, but he wasn't sure. Was it just because he had not been contacted for a while? Whatever, there was a huge doubt in his mind. Could he trust SHARP? Were they the good guys or were they just as bad as STRAP. The itch – was it because he didn't trust SHARP or, for that matter, Kaz?

There was only one way to deal with this. He would have to talk to Kaz...

As the thought formed in Danny's mind, his phone began to vibrate in his pocket. Maybe SHARP knew he was having doubts and this was Kaz now.

He pressed answer. It wasn't Kaz. It was Mark,

loud and cheerful as ever, snapping Danny out of his thoughts.

'Danny!'

'Yup.'

'It's your best mate, back from the State! Well, States.'

'Yup.'

'Flew in late last night on the red-eye from the US of A!'

'Yup?'

'Well, you sound pleased to hear from me!'

'Yup.'

'Have you missed your old buddy?'

'Yup.'

'Cool! Right, can't waste time chatting, there's someone I want you to meet. My house, fifteen minutes? Got that?'

'Yup.'

Hanging up, Danny swung off the bed and headed for the door. Once again, the SHARP question would just have to wait.

A quarter of an hour later, Danny parked his bike and was walking up Mark's drive, gravel crunching underfoot, sidling past the huge black 4X4 with the golf clubs in the back. As he reached for the doorbell the front door swung open to reveal a huge grin splashed across Mark's familiar face. He was, Danny noticed, ridiculously tanned. How did he manage to get so brown in a week?

'Raining in Florida?' asked Danny.

Mark turned up his grin a notch or two, blasting Danny with its radiance.

'Like the tan, eh?' Mark chuckled. 'All natural, buddy, not sprayed on! How was Venice?'

'Wet. Or at least the streets were.'

The boys grabbed hands and bumped shoulders in a rough greeting.

'Looking good!' said Mark.

'You too.'

'I was talking about me!'

Danny pulled a face: *bleugh*! 'Shouldn't you have jet-lag or something?' he asked.

'Nah. Slept on the plane, got home fresh. Good job too, 'cos AJ was coming to stay today.'

'AJ?'

'My cousin AJ. You know. AJ!'

Danny didn't know. He had never met AJ, though he had heard Mark mention him often enough.

'Funny I've not met him before now, seeing he's round yours so often.'

'That's why I called you,' said Mark. 'He's staying for a couple of days while his parents are away on business.'

Stepping inside the house, Danny admired, as he always did, the expensive, minimal smartness of white walls, hard floors and shiny gadgets. He loved it.

'Griff's here, back from C Parks a day early,' said Mark. 'Thought we could all hang out. Chillin', bro!'

Danny winced. It was always worse when Mark came back from the States – the rest of the time he was almost normal. He should come with his own phrasebook.

Mark led the way upstairs.

'AJ's – well, you'll see. He's *different*. And cool, really cool,' he said over his shoulder.

The heavy bass beat of a song came pulsing from one of several bedrooms that led off the landing. Mark headed for its source.

'This is AJ's room. Always has the same one, so it's kinda his.'

Danny entered and stopped dead in his tracks. The room was the neatest, tidiest place Danny had ever seen. Though Danny was compulsively tidy, even his room could not compare to this. Everything was in its place. Books on shelves, clothes on hangers, CDs in racks; everything was organised perfectly. But where Danny arranged his books by topic and size, whoever had arranged these had also put similar coloured covers together. The clothes, too, were organised by type and colour: blue shirts, then white ones, then striped and so on. Even the pictures on the wall were arranged by colour and size.

'Hey, Aje! Someone to see ya!' said Mark. 'It's my man Dan.'

By the window was a desk, with two figures leaning over something that was spread across its surface. One of them glanced up and waved a hand at Danny. It was Griff. Danny nodded back. The other boy did not look up.

'Hi,' said Danny.

AJ did not answer.

Slim, not very tall, AJ's fair hair flopped across his forehead and hid his eyes as he bent over the desk. He did not even glance at Danny as his hands flew over the surface. Danny stepped closer, intrigued. He could see now what AJ was doing – a jigsaw puzzle! The box lay on the table: five hundred pieces, a view of New York. But there was something odd. The half-completed puzzle had no picture! The spare pieces were all the same colour too, the colour of plain cardboard.

As AJ deftly clicked pieces into place, Danny realised what he was seeing. AJ was doing the jigsaw blank side up! He wasn't going by the colours or designs on each piece – just the shape. It must be amazingly difficult!

The boy was like a puzzle-solving machine! His concentration was intense, his movements swift and efficient as he slotted pieces in. Danny frowned at the shrinking group of spare pieces, unable to see where any of them fitted. AJ just motored on, unstoppable, astounding.

With only a dozen pieces left on the table, it happened. AJ hesitated, eyes wide. His fingertips tapped the top of his head rapidly as he searched for a piece, any piece, to fit into the jigsaw. As the moments stretched out, his tapping fingertips drummed faster and he began to mutter quietly, 'Where where where where where?'

Danny spotted it first. Picking up one of the spare pieces, he popped it into place. AJ looked up at him, a broad grin lighting up his face, like he was noticing Danny for the first time.

'Hi!' he said.

'Hi,' replied Danny.

'Good one!' beamed AJ.

'Thanks,' smiled Danny.

Another minute and the puzzle was finished, the last piece snapped in.

AJ looked at his watch. 'Five hundred pieces, twenty-four minutes ten seconds!' He was glowing with triumph.

'Fantastic work!' gushed Danny, amazed.

AJ peered at him from behind his floppy fringe, smiling shyly.

The afternoon flew by, the three friends hanging out with the strange, quiet AJ.

When Danny was leaving for home, Mark nodded back up the stairs towards AJ's room.

'Cool guy, eh?'

'Cool as,' agreed Danny. 'Ice cold. Doesn't say too much, though. Like he's in his own world.'

Mark nodded. 'It's called Asperger's Syndrome,' he said. 'Thinks differently from you and me, got his own way of doing things. Total genius but doesn't do communication too well. Like he was off school the day they did social skills!'

Danny jumped on his bike and pedalled for home, thinking of the cool, quirky, shy guy with such a different view of the world.

CHAPTER 3

Why Kids?

Just as Danny was swinging his bike around the corner into his street, he felt the distinctive vibration, the unique pulsing his mobile phone only ever made when SHARP was contacting him. In the brief time it took him to check it was safe to stop, then to brake to a standstill, the pulsing had stopped. He pulled out his phone.

'Damn!' Danny cursed under his breath. How typical that SHARP should try to contact him when he couldn't pick up.

Turning through his garden gate he jumped off, stowed the machine in the shed and let himself in. Unsnapping his cycle helmet he took the stairs three at a time and reached the sanctuary of his own room. He switched on his computer. Perhaps he could try again to beat that final level...

Black for a few seconds, the screen suddenly turned an intense blue and then dissolved into a swirl of flowing colours. It began to fill with text, and a button appeared at the bottom of the page marked 'post your reply'.

Hi, Danny. It's me, Kaz!
Danny, I couldn't get through to your mobile. Is there a problem?

Hi, Kaz. You rang while I was on my bike and I couldn't pick up

Oh, sorry! Still, it's better to communicate on here than on your phone. Way less expensive for us, and perhaps less likelihood of interruptions for you.

Possibly, although my sister has been known to barge into my room without knocking, so if I switch you off quick, you'll know why.

That's okay, Danny. I've got some instructions for another trip back in time. I hope you can take it - it's a great mission. I know it's been a while since we spoke.

A while? Ages!

I know, I know and I'm sorry but sometimes it gets manic here. You know how much trouble we've had

with STRAP.

Kaz, I don't know if I can carry on. The danger, now there's this outfit called STRAP around, seems to be on the increase. Who are they and how dangerous are they? I've got these unanswered questions in my head, Kaz, and I just can't stop stressing about it... There's something really bothering me...

What is it? Tell me. I'll do my best to answer.

Look Kaz, it's hard to explain - in fact I am not at all sure what it is but things just don't seem to add up, I mean about SHARP and STRAP. That's why I've been trying to contact you. I need answers.

Danny paused and then a sudden thought shot into his mind with incredible force. Of course, that was it what he had been trying to figure out! That was the question he couldn't pin down.

What I don't understand, Kaz, is why SHARP, and apparently STRAP, only recruit kids, quite young kids at that. I seem to be the oldest. Why not adults from the twenty-first century?

You think too much, Danny.

Kaz, that isn't an answer.

I know, and you are right to ask this question, it's just that it involves a pretty big explanation and I probably need one of the people in charge here like Professor Dobbs to answer it, but I'll try my best.
Do you remember Professor Dobbs explaining that every thought leaves a trace, what we call fracs, and that is why what happened in the past affects the future?

Yes, I certainly do.

Well, adults carry much more of those traces – their past actions, past deeds with them – and some of those traces would go back with them into the past and mess up things even more if we sent adults back. A kid is more like a 'clean slate'. In your time the disciplines of knowledge were very separate. For instance, religious thought and philosophy were not part of science or more importantly part of neurological study. That is where the break-through came in our time - the

integration of disciplines, together with technological advancements, to allow for things like time travel.

For a moment there was no response from Danny.

Does that answer your question?

Yeah, it does - but I still don't know how I feel about another mission. And if STRAP are the evil guys why do they not just use adults and cause more mayhem that way?

Danny, you are getting in deeper. The fact is: they are. What they do is send a kid back and then if the kid has detected lots of fracs, they send a pretty bad guy back and here's the bit I hadn't wanted to tell you: we get rid of those people.

You mean kill them.

So far we have been able to prevent any of them landing in the past. That little kid Sarah did so much good on her trip back, we were able to track her trajectory after you had rescued her and we knew ex-

actly where they were going to send a 21st century adult and we blew up their landing place. I do assure you that the person they had planned to send was a multiple killer.

That is serious stuff, Kaz! I now know a bit more than I wanted to, really.

But I've answered some of your questions haven't I? I've probably put you off another mission even more now.

Noooh… but I keep getting time slip whenever I travel.

We know you do Danny, but you know all about it. It's a sort of jet-lag that time-travellers get. But people get jet-lag and loads of xrosmonauts get time slip. It's just one of those things. We've told you how to get over it, haven't we?

Yes I know, and I'm not making a fuss about it. Sailors get seasickness – well, some do – and time-travellers get time slip. I'm not a wimp. I just do hate it when it comes. Look I'll have a good think about an-

other mission. You've said it's a good one. Is it far back in time? That always seems to make the jet lag worse.

You're right, it does but it's only back to World War 2.

Wow! That's tempting. I'll think about it, OK?

Sure, Danny. I'll be in touch.
Kaz

As soon as the screen faded and his own desktop replaced the SHARP configuration, Danny regretted that he hadn't given Kaz a definite 'yes' for the next mission.

The afternoon dragged. By comparison with that afternoon, glaciers raced along like Ferraris. Geography lessons (not Danny's favourite) zipped along like racehorses. Even continental drift seemed rather hasty. Running out of daft comparisons, Danny tried to distract himself. He tidied his room, quite unnecessarily. He tried to write a posting for his blog, the one SHARP had him start when he first joined them. When he read it back it was total garbage. He deleted it.

To take his mind off things, Danny sat at his computer and opened up the game he was so near to finishing – the one Jenny had caught him epic-failing on the last level. This time he got thrashed all over the screen. Noob! Giving it up, he pulled a sheet of paper and a pencil from his desk drawer and tried again with the knotty problem of his Year 9 options. That would take his mind off things. He started scribbling.

'Ahaaa!'

For the second time that day Danny nearly jumped out of his skin as Jenny sprang through his bedroom door. He glared at her irritatingly cheerful face. Jenny beamed at his irritatingly grumpy one.

'Don't you knock?'

'Yes,' Jenny replied, 'but you don't answer. I thought you might have your iPod on. Or been kidnapped by aliens. Or something.' Her grin grew wider. 'Message from Mum: *Daniel, your dinner's ready.* And message from Dad: *Tell the beast it's feeding time.*' She hesitated. 'And one from me: Are you okay, Dan?'

Jenny's grin had dropped. Danny wished she would pick it back up; it was as though she had put a light out. She tilted her head to one side like an attentive hen, waiting for an answer.

'Mum's called you about three times. Didn't you hear her?'

'Really? No, sorry, I didn't. I was just...' He

waved vaguely at the sheet of paper on the desk.

'Trying to work out your options?'

'You could say that.'

'I just did.' The grin was back. 'You're a real man of mystery, aren't you?'

That smile, Danny thought was laced with the tiniest hint of suspicion.

'Anything I can help with?' she offered.

'Nope.' Danny flopped back in his chair. 'I'll be right down.'

Jenny turned to go. She might be a bit of a pain at times, but at least she knew when to leave well alone.

'Sis!'

She turned back.

'Thanks for asking.' Danny screwed up the paper in his hand; there wasn't anything useful on it anyway. 'But I've just got to do some thinking.'

'Don't strain yourself!' she said, dodging out of the door to avoid the expected flying paper ball.

As Danny sat down at the table, Mr and Mrs Higgins exchanged meaningful glances and for a moment Danny was afraid he was in for one of their 'concerned parent' sessions. For a while it looked like he'd get away with it: Simon Higgins talking university stuff, Rachel talking health centre stuff, both talking history stuff.

Then Mr Higgins cleared his throat.

'Erm - you alright, old man?'

'Me?' asked Danny.

'Mmm, you,' replied his dad.

'Alright?'

'Yes. Are - you - alright?' Mr Higgins spoke slowly, patiently, as though English might not be his son's first language.

Danny realised that everyone was gazing at him.

'You're not your usual positive self.' Mr Higgins fingered the knot of his tweed tie. 'Normally you eat like a starved bear but you're just sitting there, rearranging peas. Are you *quite* sure you're well, old man?'

Suddenly self-conscious at how much attention he had attracted, Danny slapped on a grin.

'Yes, thank you. Perfectly well,' He started shovelling up man-sized forkfuls of lasagne.

His mum laid a concerned hand on his elbow. 'Year 9 options still a worry?'

Danny smiled non-committally.

'You know,' his dad said, 'sometimes you can think too hard about something. Things generally turn out alright anyway. Remember when we got lost looking for Stonehenge? We still had a super day out.'

Danny remembered. On the way back home from a week in the Isle of Wight, a wrong turn out of Southampton, endless hours bimbling through Dorset and Hampshire...

'Or those road works on the way back from London? Without that we'd never have seen Watling Street!'

Oh yes, Danny remembered that, too. Up the M1 at Dad's usual steady 45mph, everything else streaking past them, then another wrong turn that sent them miles up the A5 through Milton-flipping-Keynes. Another turn-off, Jenny carsick, Dad waving at the road sign labelling the dull stretch of grey tarmac as Watling Street, hub of the Roman British road system. Wrong turns. Bimbling about. Not great examples, Dad!

'Take a day off, Danny. Do something else. Then think about it again and things'll seem much clearer.'

'And if they don't dear, we're always here to help,' added his mum.

Danny nodded appreciation and forced a smile. But most of his attention was on his mobile, which had started pulsing silently with the insistent rhythm that only came with calls from SHARP.

Kaz!

CHAPTER 4

Top Brass

Zipping up the stairs Danny shot into his room, turning the lock. He pulled out his phone. The screen lit up blue, sliding away and expanding to the size of a TV panel. Floating in the air just in front of him, colours swirling across it, its carbon-black edge was clear, sharp. But it wasn't Kaz.

Good evening, Danny. I don't believe we've spoken before. My name is Professor Bucephalus Crumpshall, Senior Professor. It is my privilege to meet you.

Danny's eyes lingered on the words 'Senior Professor'. He tapped in his reply and hit 'send'.

Pleased to meet you, Professor Crumpshall.

Please, call me 'Bertie': everyone does. Danny, I know you have had a discussion today with Kazaresh Porterman - Kaz. Quite a difficult conversation, I believe. One which requires the input of someone senior.

Yes, Bertie. So are you the senior professor at SHARP? The head, the top man?

Danny, I understand you are having doubts about your work as a SHARP agent. You are also experiencing feelings of confusion, uncertainty, impatience. Is that correct?

Yes. But are you...

You feel that SHARP has not been entirely frank with you, you think you may be at risk, but you do not wish to stop time travelling. This gives rise to feelings of conflict. You are also suffering from loss of concentration and appetite. Correct?

Correct. But...

Danny, I have agreed to assist in your case as I believe I know what is the matter with you. I can help you.

Danny stared at the screen, puzzled. This guy seemed really concerned about him. Obviously Kaz must have said that he had been a bit unsure about carrying on.

First, SHARP has not shown the correct appreciation of your talents. I feel you should be rewarded for your work. Paid, perhaps. Or allowed to bring back ancient objects from your missions, items which you could then sell as valuable antiques.

I thought xrosmonauts weren't encouraged to bring things back from the past. Kaz said it was too expensive, used too much energy.

I think we might stretch a point for you. After all, you are one of SHARP's most skilled and valuable agents. Perhaps the best.

Thank you!

It is we who should be thanking you, Danny. And so, my second suggestion: the award of a medal for outstanding service.

Oh right, a medal. Fantastic!

Danny tried to put some enthusiasm in his voice. SHARP seemed to be fond of this medal idea. They had awarded one to Sarah Lacey and he had been happy to pass it on to her. But she was a nine-year-old kid and, of course, she'd been pleased, though goodness knows how she had explained it to her mum and dad. But he was well past the 'good-work' sticker stage by now.

And you have already received the honour of using the letters 'Xr' after your name, the first two letters of our word 'xrosmonaut', showing your successful completion of two time trips. So I ask: Will you continue to travel in time for SHARP?

I have been thinking seriously about it.

Why wasn't he saying 'Yes' straight away? He had been so keen just a few minutes ago – anxious to hear back from Kaz.

Your feelings of suspicion and confusion, not being quite yourself: I promise to think about those further. And I fully understand that we have not communicated well with you in the past.

You can say that again. I've tried to contact SHARP lots of times

Well, yes – we will try to do better, much better, in the future. I'll meet with you and help clear everything up. You'll find we are **much** more communicative in future.

Great. Thank you so much.

My pleasure. All I ask is that you think about what I have said, and about working for SHARP again. No need to answer now - you will be contacted again soon. Goodbye, Danny Higgins.

Bye.

The floating screen immediately shrank back to fit its normal space on the mobile.

Danny felt better. *Much* better. In fact, now he thought of it, his mum had made one of her special apple crumbles for desert – she'd been rummaging in the oven for it when he'd suddenly nipped upstairs. And she had probably made her super-thick, stand-your-spoon-up custard. He could definitely manage a dessert. He sauntered downstairs and smiled happily at everyone, banishing their worries.

Filled with apple crumble and a sense of wellbeing, Danny slept soundly that night, until he was woken suddenly at 3.30am. He reached under his pillow realising that what had woken him was the steady, pulsing vibration from his phone – SHARP's trademark signal. He felt wide awake, ready for anything, much more the old Danny.

He tapped the phone on. Again, the screen detached, hovering silently just in front of him, expanding in brilliant colours as the message text came through.

Hi Danny. It's me, Kaz. It's about the conversation earlier, about you working for SHARP.

Hi, Kaz, mate. Good to hear from you! Look, I've thought about this – working for SHARP, and the discussion earlier. I'll do it: I'll do the mission, if it's still on offer.

Wow! Danny, I didn't expect that! That's brilliant! Yes, the mission's still available. It's right up your street. And it's a vital one, Danny. We need someone excellent - we need you.

You've got me.

Good! Look, it's a while since you've done a mission, so I've got to give you the travel instructions again. I'll patch them through now and the mission brief will follow...

The text faded, the vivid colours swirling hypnotically. Then ...

‹Welcome once again Danny TO SHARP 15798›
SHARP Instructions and Policy.

‹Policy Information›
You have a full copy of our policy. It has not changed. We still hold firm in the belief that it is possible to travel back safely through time to bring about the greater good of all humanity past and present.

‹Pre-Travel Information›
You will notice that we have changed the pulse of our initial communication to you, but you will still recognise that it is different from the usual one for your phone. Our modifications on your new phone now take account of the new technology provided by your iPhone. Instead of black, green and red buttons, you

have, of course, the phoenix icons: black for information such as our contact at the moment; green for when you want to take up an option to travel back in time which you follow up by keying in your project number 15798. When it is time for us to facilitate your return to the twenty-first century you will feel your phone vibrating and you can then press the red phoenix and key in your project number. Just as before, you can press the red phoenix to return any time you are experiencing real danger. But try to remember this is for real emergencies.

‹Travel Information›

We cannot emphasise enough the importance of being alone and somewhere safe before setting out, and of no one missing you. We are still aiming at our young 21st century time travellers only being away from their own time for four to six minutes. This allows for several hours or possibly days in the time they have travelled back to. However, under difficult conditions, the time you are away in your present might be longer. Because of this, try to make absolutely sure no one is likely to notice or be worried by your absence.

You know that it is more difficult, though not impossible,

for us to transport bodies wearing clothes, so 'strip down to underpants whenever possible' is still the instruction.

Our material scientists have been working wonders with the travel bag and it is now lighter and more flexible than ever. When it is stuck to your side, you really will not feel it. Remember to do this before you leave. We have had trouble with a time traveller forgetting to put the camera disc on their forehead and so the whole journey was a waste of time, power and money because nothing was recorded! So remember, on arrival, however dreamy or dozy you feel, (and we do know this is one of the effects) take the silver disc out and press it to your forehead. When the backing disc comes away leaving just the film, do put this back in the bag. These discs are actually quite expensive and can be re-used.

‹After Your Visit›

We will, of course, contact you after your trip to let you know how you have done. We are extremely pleased with your blog Danny. It is gaining interest around the world and it maybe that you will help us to recruit others from different countries or continents through your work. We have noted your confusion about the rogue outfit STRAP which you have expressed on your blog. Hopefully you will come to understand that they are the ENEMY.

Current travel options will follow...

‹Details of Current Travel Option›

‹Time Zone›
3rd May 1926.

‹Place›
Dorset, England: just outside Wimborne.

‹Landing›
Outbuildings at The Green Man public house.

‹Instructions›
Change into the clothes of the period and take the bicycle.

‹Destination›
The road outside. Wait: your contact will be riding a bicycle and will find you.

<Conditions>

Favourable. Weather benign. No war or disease risk. Some social unrest.

<Identity>

Grocer's delivery boy.

<Equipment>

Mobile phone, travel bag. Mobile phone with beam of light activated when t-o-r-c-h is keyed in (only use sparingly).

If you wish to travel, do as follows:

›   Take off your clothes, except for underpants.

›   Press the time/space travel bag close to your body so that it is attached.

›   Press the green phoenix icon on your mobile and enter the project number 15798.

Good luck with this vital mission.

Danny read over the familiar instructions and the new mission briefing. It felt comfortable but exciting. His doubts were gone: he was ready. Reaching up to the shelf over his bed, he found the elephant-shaped money box that he didn't use but couldn't throw away because it had been a present from Gran and that he now told himself was cool, kitsch art! Tucked behind it, as always, he found the small, flat space/time travel bag. What weird physics did SHARP use to get it there? He never saw the bag arrive and never saw SHARP retrieve it after each trip; didn't know how they did it, and now he didn't care. He was about to step through time again and the thought thrilled him to the core of his bones.

Slipping off the tee-shirt and shorts that he slept in, Danny pulled on a pair of underpants. He pressed the travel bag to his tummy where it stuck firmly, like it was part of him. Determined now and keen to go, Danny picked up his mobile, pressed the green phoenix and keyed in 15798. He heard a faint high-pitched whine, far off but coming nearer. Then... Nothing.

It wasn't a bump, the landing, merely a change in the texture and resistance of the surface under Danny's bare feet, from the carpet of his bedroom to hard flagstones. As though the ground rose to meet him.

Opening his eyes, Danny blinked in the gloom. Motes of dust drifted in the warm air, which was filled with the richly delicious scent of sawn, sappy wood mixed with damp earth and machine oil. Bars of light streamed through the gaps round the edge of a rough door set high in the wall above, cutting the dimmer beams that leaked in round closed wooden shutters below.

It seemed to be some sort of storeroom, a cross between a barn and a toolshed. Rusting tools hung on nails in one wall, where a few hay bales were piled neatly. Battered paint tins stood on a makeshift shelf, dabs of colour revealing their contents. One end of the building was stacked with crates of empty brown bottles and several large wooden barrels.

Slipping his mobile into the travel bag, Danny took out the silver recording disc and pressed it to his forehead, feeling the backing come away as the device dissolved into his skin.

Now where are these clothes?

He found them instantly, draped over the frame of a big black bicycle that was propped against a clean-scrubbed, rough wooden table. On the table stood a large, round cheese wrapped in thin, white muslin cloth, several jars of pickled onions and a brown paper sack full to the brim with apples.

Danny dressed quickly: itchy, knitted, brown

woollen socks, a long-sleeved shirt of thickish white cotton and dark brown, button-up trousers that had elastic braces. Danny looped the braces over his shoulders. He laced on heavy, black ankle-boots, rolling up his shirtsleeves, thinking it was too warm for the tweed jacket and then put on the long, blue-striped apron and the flat tweed cap.

SHARP's mission brief had instructed him to take the bicycle. That must mean the one lent against the table, he thought.

It was a grocer's delivery bike, black and solid. The steel plate on the crossbar bore the name of 'John Curtis, Family Grocer and Provision Merchant, Wimborne'. Its hard leather saddle was cracked and worn. Oddly, the front wheel was a good span smaller than the back one, leaving room for the huge wicker basket that hung in front of the curved back handlebars. Danny bundled up the jacket and stowed it in the empty basket. A battered enamel badge gave the bike-maker's name: *Hercules.*

Danny pulled the bike upright. It weighed a ton!

Oof! You'd have to be Hercules to lift this thing! Wheeling the bike towards the door, he was reaching for the iron latch when...

SLAM! The door flew open, revealing a red-faced, red-haired boy of about his own age. The lad stopped, grinned, looked Danny up and down, then threw back his head and yelled.

'Zin 'ere, maister! 'Ees jus' a-stannin' loike 'eez a-stogged, the nogger'ead!'

CHAPTER 5

Sudden Contact

Danny looked blankly at the grinning boy.

Had the time jump affected his hearing – or maybe his brain? How was he going to function in 1926 if he could understand hardly a word anyone said? Then it went dark, for the man who stepped up behind the red-haired lad was so broad that his bulk filled the doorway, almost blocking out the daylight.

'Be off with ye, Tom, an' don't you scold 'im loike that! Bustin' in on the chap! You get about yer work!' Tom scrambled round him and through the door. 'An' you speak the King's English when you're roun' the pub – you ain't on the farm now, y'know!'

Did people in Dorset really used to speak like Tom? Danny hoped there weren't too many who did!

'Don't you mind Tom, lad – daft as a brush but harmless. Thinks 'es all growed up cos 'es fourteen and left school!'

The big man stuck his thumbs behind his broad braces. Behind him, Tom did the same, still grinning.

'I wuz lookin' for you, son. You must be that grocer's new lad. Tom said 'e'd seen you ride up on that boike o'yours 'n disappear in 'ere.'

Ambling in, the big man laid a huge hand on Danny's shoulder. His balding head shone, his baggy black trousers strained over an ample waistline and his white shirtsleeves were bloused above the elbow by springy metal armbands. As he brushed past Danny he smelled of beer and something musty, like an old rug.

'Let's have a look-see what you brought us, then.' He ran his paw-like hand over the goods on the table.

'Cheese, onions, apples – all there. Good lad! You tell your gaffer that Charlie Witchet, that's me, Charlie's right pleased with this stuff. What with all the commotion goin' on, folk have been buying in panic and the shops are running short. We'll be busy today, 'n' some folk'll wanna be fed, so I'm proper grateful for the d'livery. Tell your gaffer I'll send my Tom into town t'morrow to settle his bill like we agreed, eh lad?'

'Yes, Mr Witchet,' Danny nodded, turning to leave.

'Hey, not so fast!' the big man called sharply.

Danny froze.

'You been riding that boike around all day, I 'spect, what with all the commotion. 'Ere lad, this is for you. Like I said, I'm proper grateful.'

He pulled something out of his pocket and handed it to Danny, who looked at it blankly – it was a small silver coin, like a ten-pence piece.

'Whassamatter, lad, never seen a bob before?' the man chuckled.

'A bob?'

'Aye lad, a bob! A shilling. Twelve pennies. That's for you. Not the first tip you've had today, eh?'

Danny smiled. 'No, sir. Thank you very much, sir!'

He slipped the coin into his pocket where it chinked against others. He had no idea what it was worth but thought he had better look grateful. He turned to go.

'Ere, lad – you been nicking my apples?'

Danny froze again.

The big fellow was grinning.

'Just my little joke, lad. 'Ere – and a couple for later.'

He took an apple from the sack on the table, then two more, and threw them. Danny caught them skilfully and tucked them into his bike basket.

'Thanks!'

As he pushed his bike out through the door the

big man's voice carried past him, booming, 'Tom! Get in here an' move these empties for the drayman!' Tom scurried in.

Danny found himself in the yard of a pub, a red brick building with a double-peaked roof of clay tiles. A painted sign read *The Green Man*. A tree-lined road ran past the yard entrance, with low cottages close by. He pushed the bike up to the road, its turning wheels *tick-tick-tick*-ing. He could hear the distant bleating of sheep, and from the outbuilding came the hollow drumming of wooden barrels being shifted, the muffled rattle and clash of empty bottles as Charlie and Tom moved the crates.

It was ages before anything came along the road. At first there was no traffic at all, then a large, flat wagon drawn by two huge, hairy-hoofed horses made its slow way up to the pub and turned into the yard, the draymen loading up empty barrels and crates then going back the way they had come. People began to make their way along the road to the pub, most on foot. A few were on bicycles but they disappeared inside the pub yard, so none of those could be his contact. Only one car passed by, a big brown car with a cloth roof, a shiny grille and wheels with spokes. Danny grinned. A vintage car – but brand new! He just caught the name as it motored past; it was a *Crossley*, a marque he'd never heard of.

In the distance, a church clock chimed six. As the sixth chime faded on the breeze a bicycle turned into the road, its rider pedalling hard. The bike seemed too big, as though it had been bought for him to grow into. It was a lighter version of Danny's delivery bike, a touring bicycle with equal-sized wheels, a small basket up front and a leather saddlebag behind, both stuffed full. The rider was a boy; Danny could see that now. It was a schoolboy. He could make out an old-fashioned school cap, shorts, long socks and a rumpled blazer. As the boy pedalled he was looking left, right, up at the sky, at the pub, in fact everywhere except where he was going!

Danny watched him approach. This daydreaming kid couldn't be his contact, could he? Danny looked up and down the road, to see if anyone else was coming from another direction. No cars, no people, no bikes, so this must be his...

CRASH!

Danny's feet were knocked from under him and the next moment he was on the ground, tangled up with the schoolboy and his bicycle. He had pedalled straight into him! The two boys and their machines rolled in a tangled heap.

'I say, w-watch where you're going!' the boy shrilled from behind his cap, which had slipped across his face.

'Me?!' huffed Danny. 'But you rode into me, I was just standing there!'

'In the r-road, you nuisance!' twittered the boy. 'You're a danger to traffic, that's what you are!'

'*Me*?!' hooted Danny, incredulous.

'Yes, *you*! There's nobody else down here, is there?'

'Well I wish there was,' said Danny, 'because then they could untangle us!'

For a moment the schoolboy was still. Then his shoulders began to shake silently. An odd wailing sound seeped from behind the cap. For a dreadful moment Danny thought the boy was crying. Then the sound turned into a weird, high-pitched crowing noise and the cap slipped off his face. The boy was laughing! His face was screwed up tight, his extraordinary braying laugh grating the air. Danny couldn't help joining in and soon the two boys were rolling about in helpless mirth, as though a bike crash was just the funniest thing in the world! Catching their breath, the two untangled limbs and machines and climbed to their feet.

'You alright?'

'Aaaaah – yes, thanks, s-still in one piece,' said the boy.

'You've scuffed your knee.' Danny pointed to a thin trickle of blood oozing from the leg of the boy's baggy shorts.

'Aaaaah – y-yes, I j-jolly well have, haven't I?' The lad dabbed his knee with a none-too-clean handker- chief and chuckled.

'Does it hurt?' inquired Danny, concerned.

'Hurt? Ah-ah-ah – no, doesn't hurt at all. Don't really feel these things usually.'

'*Usually*? Do this sort of thing much, do you?'

'Mmm, 'fraid s-so. Walk into things, ah-ah-ah, fall off things, trip over … well, you know how it is.'

Danny didn't know how it was – he wasn't at all accident-prone or uncoordinated – but he didn't say so. As the schoolboy straightened up his bike, picked up his stuff and brushed the dust from his clothes, Danny was able to get a closer look at him.

He was a bit – well, *different*! Shortish and quite skinny, with bony knees, angular limbs and swarthy skin. A broad face with a snub nose, heavy brows, pink ears that stood out, all topped by a mop of brown, short-back-and-sides hair that flopped over from a side-parting.

The boy looked up, apparently not sure whether to smile or not. He peered at Danny from under long, dark eyelashes: his eyes were a startling blue, with the rich brightness of stained glass.

'Aah-ah-ah-S-sorry about that.'

His strangely high-pitched voice was posh in that cut-glass way you hear in old black-and-white films, but there was also that 'ah-ah-ah' thing, and falling over his words: what was that? Not *exactly* a stammer, but a sort of hesitation. And something else too – a far-away look, as though he was gazing out from behind a thick sheet of glass.

'Y-You're s-staring.'

It was true, Danny had been.

'Sorry,' said Danny. 'No offence meant, it's just that you remind me of someone I know. I just can't think who it is. But you *should* be more careful, you know – you could get hurt on the road, not paying attention like that.'

The boy looked down at his shoes, shuffling and frowning deeply. Suddenly he looked quite small and vulnerable. Now the shock of the crash had sunk in, he also looked upset.

'No harm done, anyway,' said Danny quickly. 'Let's start again, shall we? My name's...'

He paused: SHARP hadn't given him a name to use on this mission. What name should he use? Nobody had told him the name of the delivery boy whose place in space and time Danny was now occupying. But this kid didn't sound local, so maybe he wouldn't know the difference anyway.

'I'm Danny.'

The boy said nothing, still shuffling his feet.

'Let's get moving, before that knee of yours gets stiff, eh?'

The boy nodded. They started to walk slowly in the direction the boy had been riding, away from *The Green Man* and the cottages and out of town.

'So what's your name, then?' asked Danny. No answer.

He tried again, with his best matey grin.

'Where are you off to on that bike, apart from finding people to crash into?'

The boy just sniffed. As an effort to cheer the kid up it wasn't going too well!

'I'm touring,' the boy mumbled.

'Touring?' Well, the lad was on a touring bike. The boy held out his hand for Danny to shake. Danny shook it. No name, but he's touring. Well, at least that's something!

CHAPTER 6

Touring By Bicycle

They walked on in silence, strides lengthening as the boy walked off the stiffness in his grazed knee. Danny didn't want to push the boy for his name. Though at first neither the crash nor his wounded knee had seemed to bother him, now the poor kid looked really worried about something. Danny tried again.

'So, where did you start your trip – touring?'

I started mine in 2012, he thought, and here I am eighty-six years back in time, with a contact SHARP has wanted me to make – a weepy kid!

'Ah-ah-ah – F-France,' said the boy, looking Danny squarely in the face. If it killed him, he wasn't going to show he was upset. Danny respected him for it; maybe he wasn't the wimp he'd thought.

'You don't sound French.'

'I'm not. My family lives there, in Dinard.'

'So are you out with your family or a cycling club or something?'

'N-no, just me,' the boy sniffed. 'I *am* nearly four-teen, you know. I set out this morning.'

'All the way from France?!'

Danny was astonished. This was the middle of Dorset, yet this small boy had come all that way in a single day, on his bike, alone. Small boy? Hang on, he was almost the same age as Danny! He seemed so much smaller and younger, though. Danny's protective parents only ever allowed him to ride a few miles, and then only when the roads were quiet, but 1920s roads were much less busy than those of the twenty-first century.

'That's a long way to come just for a bike ride!'

'Aaaah – b-but it's not just a bike ride. Oh, no.'

Intelligent blue eyes darting, the boy's quirky smile flickered back.

'Aaaah-I-I'm going to school.'

'All the way from France? On a bike? Alone?'

The boy's answer came out in one long breath.

'Yes, well you see, first there was the St Malo boat. Then there was the strike and no trains or buses and the baggage master's got my bags. Then there was the map and the telegram but what with the repairs and lunch and the pedal and the apple and the ditch and everything and it's all so beastly.'

The boy stopped dead, chest heaving, gasping in great gulps of air, frowning hard.

Danny stopped too. The kid was getting really uptight now, but had Danny just touched a nerve or was it something more serious? He had said he was touring; now he said he was going to school. So which was it? And what was all that stuff he'd gabbled – the muddle of disconnected words that lay before Danny like the jumbled pieces of a puzzle?

A puzzle... a puzzle...

Hey, I know who he reminds me of!

It was Mark's cousin, AJ; the boy who did jigsaws back side up. In many ways they were so different, but there was something about the way the boy's quick mind showed through those inward-looking eyes, something in the way he spoke. So like AJ, the cool and quirky guy with Asperger's Syndrome. What did Mark say about AJ? Thinks differently from you and me – got his own way of doing things, like he was off the day they did social skills! That fitted this boy perfectly: so maybe he had Asperger's too? He had to help him. Not because of the Asperger's or because he reminded him of AJ, although he did. It was just that, he deserved his help.

Reality cut into Danny's thoughts. He realised that the boy was no longer walking at his side. He had stopped a few paces back. He stood still, looking ahead up the road, then back the other way, over and over. Then he seemed to make up his mind.

'Well,' he said matter-of-factly, 'I'm going home.'

He wheeled his bicycle round and started to walk back the way they had come.

Danny was flabbergasted. Home?! It seemed so wrong that after coming all this way this gutsy guy should give it all up and head for home, all the way back to France! Why? What was the matter with him?

'Hang on a minute,' he called, 'I need your help.'

The boy stopped and turned, blinking. 'M-*My* help? Whatever for?'

'Well,' said Danny cheerily, 'all that stuff about boats and bags and maps and schools, really. I mean you just sort of blurted it all out and you didn't finish explaining, so I didn't really understand what you were talking about. Well, not properly. And I'm a bit obsessive about things like that – I hate not understanding things.'

'Really?' The boy's eyes widened. 'Me too! It drives me *barmy*!'

'See? We're quite similar really,' smiled Danny. 'So you're not going to rush off without explaining it all to me, are you? I'm interested. And if you've got a problem, telling someone might help.'

The boy's brows creased into a frown as he thought it over. Danny pressed his advantage.

'Let's pull in here for a bit.'

The boys turned their bikes off the rough road, which rose gently past a huddle of low stone buildings, some thatched, one topped by a cross. A sign announced them as St Margaret's Chapel and Almshouses. They leaned their heavy machines against the rough stones of the old church and perched on the weather-bleached gate.

'So what's the story?' asked Danny.

The boy drew a deep breath. 'Ah-ah-ah – well, I'm supposed to be on my way to my new school.'

'That your school uniform?' Danny grinned at the boy's creased and dusty clothes.

'No, it's my old school uniform – Hazelhurst School, in Sussex. I've left there now, but Mother said I should wear it one last time and save my good clothes! Good job, too – what a frightful state I'm in! Ran my bike into a ditch earlier...'

'Two accidents in one day?'

The boy didn't seem to hear Danny.

'I'm to be a new boy at Sherborne School.'

'Where's that?'

The boy frowned. 'Sherborne, oddly enough.

Here in Dorset. You do know your own county, don't you?'

'Of course. Just making sure you meant *that* Sherborne,' Danny bluffed. 'So what's it like?'

'Ah-ah-ah, I don't know yet. But it's a public school, very old. And my house-master is to be Mr O'Hanlon. I'm to be in Westcott House, so we're all in black and white clothes. The boys in different houses wear different coloured togs. And I'm to board – that means live in school – with lots of other boys, but I've not met anyone yet. Everything else is still a bit of a mystery.' Eyes fixed on a drifting cloud, his voice trailed away.

Danny couldn't imagine going to a school where you lived in. He said so.

'Oh, I'm used to it – I lived in at Hazelhurst. Not so bad after the first term. Ah-ah-Anyway, today's the first day of t-term at Sherborne and I'm due to s-start tomorrow. Mother and Daddy sent me off to the ferry this morning in St Malo – that's in France – to cross to Southampton, with my luggage and my bicycle. But when the boat landed at Southampton there were no trains or buses, so what's a chap to do but hop on the old bike and start pedalling?'

Danny was puzzled. 'Why don't you just go to

school in France?'

'Oh, n-no, that wouldn't do at all! Only an English school will do. Mother and Daddy think we should have a good English education, you see. '

'Who's 'we'?'

'Ah-ah-ah m-my brother John and me. He's four years older than me. He's at Marlborough College.'

'So why aren't you going there too? Why Sherborne School?'

'I s-say, you ask a lot of questions, don't you?'

'Only way to learn,' smiled Danny. 'You don't ask, you don't find out.'

The boy raised his eyebrows, pondering.

'Y-Y-You like learning?' The boy seemed surprised that a mere grocer's delivery boy could admit to such a thing.

'Yup, I do. Every day's a school day, I say. Never stop learning, it's what makes life interesting.'

'That's what I think too!' squeaked the boy, blue eyes sparkling. His smile faded. 'Though it's not what most of the Hazelhurst boys thought.' He chewed his lip.

'Problems?' asked Danny. 'Bullied? That why your parents moved you?'

'Oh, n-no, not at all! But I never really s-seemed

to f-fit in. I like maths and science and things. The teachers let me do experiments and read my own books, but they didn't really teach much about the things I like. And I like learning and reading about how things work and solving problems and inventing, so the other fellows thought I was a swot. They all liked sports and games. They joked that while they were playing hockey I was standing watching daisies grow!' He giggled. 'But I've invented a typewriter and a new sort of fountain pen. It dribbles a bit, but it works.' As he warmed to his theme, the curious boy's stammer had disappeared. 'Anyway, what I mean is I like thinking.'

'Nothing wrong with that. Me too,' said Danny.

'One of my favourite books,' the boy urged, 'says our bodies are like machines, but far more complicated than any machine ever built.' He scratched his nose and pushed the thick floppy hair off his forehead. 'One day I'll invent a machine that can think.'

'What will it think about?'

'Ah-ah-Everything! My machine will do all the hard work for us. We'll be free to dream and invent and learn.' He fell silent. 'Do you believe me?'

'Yeah,' grinned Danny. 'Yeah, why not? A think-ing machine would be great. Maybe it could tell me the answer to the question I asked you.'

'W-What question?'

'Why Sherborne School and not your brother's school?'

'Ah-ah-M-most public schools concentrate on Latin and Greek and ancient stuff. I don't try much with things I don't enjoy. I get a bit lost in my own head. Mother says those schools wouldn't be right for me, that I need the right school to bring me on. She says I'm 'different'.'

'You are,' said Danny. 'You're you. Different's good.'

'And Mother knew somebody at Sherborne and she said it'd be better for me. She thinks Sherborne's different too, that they might sort of let me get on with it. Better for this.' He tapped his head.

'How far have you got left to ride?'

'Thirty-one miles, roughly. Wimborne's about half-way between Southampton and Sherborne. I've been a bit slow, what with my bike breaking down and me falling off.'

Danny looked at the sky. It would be dark in a couple of hours. Thirty-one miles seemed a long way to cover in that time.

How could the boy go on in the pitch dark on

unlit country roads?

'Aaah-I was s-supposed to be staying the night at The Crown Inn in Blandford. That's about nine miles further on.'

'So you'll be there in an hour.'

'No I won't. I said before I'm not going. I'm tired, I'm alone, I don't know these roads and I'm getting hungry. No: I'm going home.'

The words stung Danny like a smack in the face. He couldn't let it happen: for some reason, deep in his mind he absolutely knew that the boy must, *must* get to his new school, as though something momentous depended on that one sole event. Kaz had said that this was an important mission. He had not explained why but somehow he knew it was about getting this boy to Sherborne school.

He thought hard, mind racing.

'Why don't I come with you?'

'T-T-To France?'

'No, to Blandford. Look, you said you're tired: it's only nine miles – much nearer than France! And you said you're hungry: well so am I but I've got some apples if you'd like one.'

The boy's face lit up. 'I love apples – they're my special favourite!'

Danny dug out a couple of apples from the basket at the front of the bike, handing the boy one and crunching into the other himself. For a minute or two they sat and chomped in friendly silence. The boy ate the core and pips too!

Licking apple juice off his lips, the boy murmured, 'What if this new school's like the old one?'

'Well, you'll find out soon enough, won't you?' said Danny, keen not to let the boy think about things too much. 'Don't give up. You're not on your own. And you're strong: no reason not to go to school. Come on, let's get moving.'

CHAPTER 7

Audentes Fortuna Juvat

The miles rolled away beneath the *tick-tick*ing wheels of the bicycles as the two boys rode on together. After a while, the boy started chattering on cheerfully, all notion of returning to France forgotten. He could talk for England! And wow, the stuff that interested him!

As well as wanting to build the thinking machine that he had mentioned earlier, he had plans for a telescope to watch the stars. And a rocket 'like that fellow Goddard did in March'. And to discover a comet, which he'd name after himself. And do some horribly complicated maths thing that went right over Danny's head, though the boy explained it three times. Then he described family seaside holidays filled with the sound of seagulls 'quockling' (his invented word for their noise: he was quite proud of it). Long drives in the French countryside, the roads straight and tree-lined just like this one. Danny got him off that subject fast, before the homesickness kicked in again!

Danny's ears pricked up at something he half-heard among the babble of good-humoured chatter.

'What was that again?'

'Ah-ah-Yes, the strike. That's why I couldn't get a bus or a train to Sherborne. Weren't you listening?'

'Course I was. I was just thinking about something,' Danny bluffed cheerfully. 'Run it past me again. The chap at the pub mentioned a strike, but I didn't really take it in.'

The boy screwed up his nose and harrumphed. 'You really will have to listen more carefully, you know. Where have you been living – in a cave?'

No, thought Danny, in the twenty-first century. He let it go: so much like AJ, this guy really must have been absent the day they did social skills!

'I was explaining,' the boy said slowly, 'that the strike is the reason I'm having to cycle to school. There are no buses or trains. All on strike. There was one bus to Salisbury but that's miles from school and they won't carry bicycles, so I'd have been stuck there.'

'What a pain!'

'Wh-When I got off the boat at Southampton I'd no choice but to cycle. I paid the station baggage master to send my luggage on to school, bought a map, sent a telegram to let school know I was on the way, and off I went. Luckily Mother had packed some basic things for me on the bike. Stopped on the way for lunch and some bike repairs, which slowed me down a bit.'

'And a couple of crashes, too!' Danny teased.

The boy giggled but his logic was ruthless. He had to get to school. If there was no public transport, there was no choice but to cycle, however far. He really did see the world differently.

As they rounded a broad bend in the road, Danny caught a faint sound drifting on the breeze. It sounded like old-fashioned nineteen-twenties jazz, the sort of thing his dad would play from his collection of old black discs when he thought nobody was listening.

'This strike, what's it all about?' asked Danny.

The boy rummaged in his saddlebag. 'This'll explain it.'

He pulled out a crumpled newspaper, pedalled closer and handed it to Danny. Under the title *The Daily Mail: Continental Edition* the banner headline blared news about the 'Great Strike'.

'M-Most people are calling it the General Strike, though' said the boy, 'because it's, well, general – that is, all the workers have been told to strike. It starts today.'

'But those people were working at the pub back there.'

'Ah-ah-It's mostly industry and public services that are affected – mines, transport, that sort of thing. People are afraid there'll be chaos and the country will collapse and there'll be a revolution or something.'

Danny pondered, listening absentmindedly to the cheerful jazz music that seemed to be drawing closer.

'Why are they striking?'

'It's all to do with the trade unions. You see…'

Danny didn't see. In fact he saw nothing but the huge, open-topped bus that, at that very moment, came hurtling around the bend and was on them in an explosive blare of jazz music and a deafening screech of horn, brakes and tyres.

Danny never really understood how he didn't end up under that bus, but thought it must have been the automatic protection shield SHARP fitted to their agents' mobiles. The driver wasn't watching the road that was for sure: as he came round that bend he was looking behind him, laughing and waving a bottle of beer. All Danny knew was that he shut his eyes and flung himself sideways, ending up in a sprawl by the roadside with the bus wheel a mere hands-breadth from his head as the big vehicle slid to a halt.

There was a heartbeat's worth of silence, then an eruption of noise.

With a gasp and a roar, the passengers on the open-topped bus – called a charabanc, Danny learned later – rushed to the aid of the two boys. Prostrate on the ground, Danny gazed stunned at the wheeling blue sky and the approaching whirl of figures.

As the press of people rushed up to him, Danny's ears were hit by a blast of heavy accents, gruff voices barking their concern. It took a moment for his stunned senses to untangle the racket into words.

'Stand baaack, you lot! Give the lad some air, dammit!' A tall, thickset figure in rough tweed clothes knelt on the road, placing his hand under Danny's head with surprising care. His voice rumbled from under a huge old-fashioned walrus moustache. 'You aw'roit, boy? Take it easy there, son.'

Danny forced his eyes to focus. Mentally he checked all his limbs, his neck, his head. Everything seemed to work: nothing hurt. He half-lay, half-sat up, propped on his elbows, and shook his head like a dog. Though he was covered in road dust there was not a single mark on him.

'My friend – where's my friend?' he demanded.

Through the wheels of the charabanc, by the ditch on the far side of the road, Danny could see another huddle of people like those around him, all men in rough work clothes, caps and heavy leather boots.

Danny jumped to his feet and sprinted round the front of the charabanc. The driver sat at the wheel, stunned and silent, staring blankly ahead. On one of the seats a portable gramophone lay disregarded, the needle jolted from the groove of the jazz record, a steady hiss and *t-tick-t-tick* streaming from the big brass horn. Behind Danny a deep voice called out, 'Get George out of that blasted driver's seat afore he runs over some other beggar!' Two men rushed to the stricken George.

Diving into the back of the huddle by the ditch, Danny elbowed his way through, terrified of what he might see. With mild grunts of surprise, the men parted to let him through.

Breath whooshed from Danny's lungs in a sudden gale of relief! There was the boy, standing in the ditch safe and sound. Pulling handfuls of dry grass and leaves from his hair and clothes, he was incoherent with fury.

Some of the men who had picked him up were

retrieving his bicycle and the belongings that had been thrown out of the bicycle basket and saddlebag – a shirt, blue pyjamas, a toilet bag, a jumble of personal stuff – and which were now strewn wildly all over the place. Now they knew the boys were unhurt, some of the men were chuckling quietly.

The boy fizzed and popped with rage. 'Aah-aah-th-three! That's *three* accidents today!'

The grinning workmen sauntered back towards the charabanc, pushing back their caps and scratching their heads in relief. The men in the ditch finished loading up the boy's bike and led both it and him back up to the road. The lad didn't look any the worse for wear, except for a few more stains and creases. In ones and twos the remaining men ambled away, patting the boy on the back, wishing him well. The last man passed him a sock he had retrieved from the hedge.

'Th-Thank you.'

'Don'ou mention it, son.'

Danny smiled at the boy. 'You alright?'

He nodded. 'You?'

'Same.'

The boy set about rearranging the things stowed on his bike, pulling them out, shaking, folding, rolling, stuffing them back.

Danny felt a big hand land on his shoulder.

'No 'arm done then, son?' It was the man who had been first to his rescue. 'An' your frien' there – he aw'roit?'

'He's aw'roit – I mean alright, thank you.'

'Good show, son.'

'How's your driver? He looks awful.'

'Ol' George? Don'ou worry yerself about 'im, he'll be roit as noinepence presently. Just scared hisself 'alf to death, tha's all. Damn near took you two with 'im.' He glanced back at the bus, where the others were teasing George about his driving.

Danny nodded.

'Name's Jim.'

'Danny.'

'Can we give you lads a lift? Seems the least we can do. Where you goin'?'

'Blandford.'

'Jus' come through there, couple o' moiles back. Be happy to take you in the charabanc.' The man nodded towards the bus.

'Charabanc?'

'Aye, we hire it when we go on outings to the races – a bit different this time. 'We're goin' to a stroike rally, y'see. Makin' a day of it.'

'You're on strike? Why?'

'I'll tell you, son. Them rich mine owners have been trying to cut wages for coal miners and make 'em work longer for their pay. Well, what's this country without coal, son? Nothin'. So Mr Herbert Smith, as leads their union, says they should 'ave 'not a penny off the pay, not a minute on the day'. But the Prime Minister Mr Baldwin says they's all after a revolution like there was in Russia back in 1917 and 'e won't give in, no 'e won't. So thassit, Mr Smith says all the union folk must strike – everyone, not just miners. Now us, we're all stonecutters, quarry men, not miners, but we all gotta stick together, us workin' men, an' make the government listen. So tha's what we're gonna do. 'Owever long it takes, whatever it costs, they'll listen.'

His eyes creased in a smile.

'It's our future, son. An' yours. Who knows what that holds, eh? What do you say to a ride to Blandford?'

'No we'll be fine thanks. Be there in no time.'

'Well, best be off.' The man held out a huge right hand. Danny shook the offered hand. It was hard and rough as sandpaper.

'You moind 'ow you go, Danny.' He nodded towards the boy, who was still fussing with the belongings on his bike. 'What's your friend's name?'

Danny raised his eyebrows.

'Actually, I've no idea.'

The workman smiled again.

'You tell 'im to moind 'ow 'e goes, too.' He strolled to the back of the charabanc, climbed aboard and gave a friendly wave.

The boys stood in the road, the hum of the chara-banc engine fading in the distance and with it the good-natured shouts of the men.

'Well,' said Danny cheerfully, 'the good news is that it's only a couple of miles to Blandford! We'll be there before you know it.'

'No.'

'What do you mean, no?'

'I'm not going to Blandford. Or school. I can't. I really should have asked them for a lift.'

Danny's mouth fell open.

'We've been through all this! We agreed we'd cycle to Blandford together, you'll stay at The Crown Inn, and tomorrow you'll finish the journey to Sher-borne. Just two more miles and you can have a rest, a bath, a meal. Just two miles! *Why* won't you go?'

The cool, distant blue eyes turned on Danny.

'I didn't say I *won't* go, I said *I can't* go. There's a

difference.'

Danny grabbed a handful of hair in frustration.

'You can't go back!' He was still certain that in some fundamental way it was essential that this guy should finish his journey.

'Can't go back? No, I can't go *on*. I'll have to go back to France. My money's gone.'

'What?!'

'Ah-ah-ah-It's q-quite simple. I haven't enough money to go on, so I've got to go back. I set off with two pounds ten shillings that Mother gave me for the whole journey. This is what I've spent.'

He handed Danny a crumpled scrap of paper on which he had jotted what he had spent along the way: six shillings and sixpence on the boat; three shillings for a map; three and eightpence on food; a shilling on bicycle repairs.

'There are some other things I've not put down there yet – the baggage porter at Southampton, having my luggage sent on to Sherborne, the telegram to school. Anyway, it all comes to one pound and sixpence. So I should have one pound nine shillings and sixpence left.'

Danny shook his head. 'Why?'

'Because two pounds ten shillings take away the

pound and sixpence I've spent leaves one pound nine-and-six. It's simple arithmetic.'

For you, maybe! thought Danny. He couldn't get his head around the complicated old currency.

'So what's the problem?'

'Mother agreed with the people at The Crown that my stay would cost ten shillings.'

'You said you've one pound nine-and-six left. That's loads more than ten shillings.'

'N-No, I said I *should* have one pound nine-and-six left. But look.' He turned out the change in his pocket. 'Only n-nine shillings and sixpence.'

Danny goggled. 'Where's the other pound?'

'N-No idea. G-Gone. It might have fallen out of my pocket – I've had three accidents today! But it's not there, or in my other things.'

'Have you looked?'

'Th-That's what I was doing before. But a pound note's a big white thing, impossible to miss: no, it's simply not there.' He paused. 'Maybe one of those workmen took it.' He was matter-of-fact, no bitterness, coolly weighing logical possibilities.

'Naaah!' said Danny, incredulous. 'That can't be right!' He looked down the road after the shadow-memory of the charabanc. 'No,' he said firmly, 'You've mislaid it, that's all. It'll probably turn up in your py-jamas or something.'

'Ah-ah-ah-P-'probably' isn't definitely. And I def-initely need ten shillings for The Crown. And I'm six-pence short of ten bob. Not enough. S-So home I go.'

At that moment Danny felt the insistent pulsing of his mobile phone, tucked in its travel bag under his clothes. The signal to return to his own time. Great timing! He had to think quickly. This kid would seri-ously blow everything just because he was a few pen-nies short! Wait – it had been given to him, so surely it was his to give?

'Here. Take this.' Danny handed the boy the shiny, silver shilling the pub landlord had given him. 'You were only sixpence short: with this shilling you've enough for The Crown and a bit over.'

The boy looked awkwardly at the bright coin. 'It's yours. I can't take it.'

'You take it,' Danny smiled. 'Call it a loan if you prefer.'

'Thank you,' the boy said simply. Then, bright-ening, 'I will pay you back. I promise.'

Pay me back? Across time and space? thought Danny.

'Course you will.'

They rode their bikes a long mile to where the road crested a low hill. Below and to the right in the gathering dusk lay Blandford.

'You'll be alright from here,' said Danny.

'They say fortune favours the brave,' said the boy.

True, thought Danny.

He dug in his bike basket, pulled out the remaining apple and handed it over. 'For later.'

The boy nodded thanks. Peering from their depths, the eyes were remote again, as though watching the world from behind a sheet of glass.

'Aah-ah-I only need sixpence, you know, not a shilling. I should give you some change.'

Danny smiled. 'Keep the change.'

'Thanks, Danny.'

'You remembered my name!'

It was only as the boy pedalled away that Danny remembered: he never had found out his name. Now he'd never know it.

He watched as the bicycle gathered speed. The last mile was all downhill.

Danny pushed his bike down a farm track and into the cover of a hedge. Sure that there was nobody around, he slipped out of his clothes and folded them neatly into the basket of the delivery bike. He pulled his phone from its bag, touched the red phoenix icon and entered 15798. From far off, from the very furthest edges of hearing, there was a faint, high-pitched whine, a piercing note of shrill sound coming nearer, louder, filling his head. Then... Nothing.

CHAPTER 8

Night Caller

SHARP had excelled themselves this time.

Danny could spend hours, maybe even days, far in the past and return to find he had been gone for only a few minutes, slotted neatly back into his own time almost where he had left it. This time his bedside alarm clock showed he had been gone for less than five minutes. He dropped down on his bed. Inside his closing eyelids a whirlpool of patterns spun. The vivid blue vortex morphed like liquid into stained glass blue eyes, alert but remote. Points of light resolved into the soft sheen of a silver shilling, rotating, fragmenting into a slow-motion explosion of jigsaw pieces.

But that buzzing – why was his alarm clock buzzing at this time of night? Why...why...?

His eyelids flicked open, daylight blasting into his protesting eyes.

Not the alarm clock: the sound was his phone's ring tone, jolting him from the deep sleep that must have come the instant his head hit the pillow.

Danny put the phone to his ear.

'Danny-Dan-Danski, old buddy! What's goin' down, dude?'

'Mmm,' replied Danny, not committing himself. He could almost see the glare of Mark's toothpaste-advert grin. He buried his head under the pillow.

'Dan, man, you know what today is, doncha?'

'Nnn-nnn.'

'It's Friday, buddy! Last day of the holidays! Get over here – we got my men AJ and Griff in the place and we gonna hang out. Maxin', relaxin', nuthin' too taxin'. We be chillin' like a villain, bro!'

'Mmmnnnnn,' Danny groaned. Did anyone actually talk like that in Florida? It'd take days to wear off Mark...

'Getcha game face on, dude. See ya in ten.'

'Nnnoo?!'

'Okay, make it twenty. Nice talking to ya!'

Mark hung up. The silence was bliss.

Danny was not 'there in ten' – or even twenty.

He stood under a hot shower for ages, allowing the powerful jets of water to revive him. He felt lousy, like he was coming down with the 'flu or something: thick-headed, puffy-eyed and sluggish. It felt like someone had nicked his brain and put a lump of dough in its place. He rubbed down with the roughest towel he could find, until his skin glowed pink, then headed for the kitchen

The kitchen noise grated on his brain like fingernails down a blackboard. Crashing pots, clinking cutlery, rustling newspapers. As Danny slunk gingerly into the room, Jenny put down her slice of toast and looked at him as if he was something the cat had dragged in.

'You look awful, Danny?' she said and then went back to eating her toast.

'Oh, Danny, what's up?' His mother got up from her chair and placed her palm on his forehead. 'Are you sickening for something?' She pulled out a chair for him as though he might be too weak to do it himself.

Mr Higgins looked up from his newspaper and his eyebrows shot up. 'You do look a little ropey, old man.'

Danny smiled wanly. Outside the kitchen window, the grim sky looked as grey as he felt. Fat raindrops pelted the neighbours' roofs. His mum set down a cup of tea in front of Danny, the steam creeping into his nostrils.

'What would you like for breakfast, hmm? You do feel up to breakfast, don't you?'

Danny always felt up to breakfast – even now, when he felt like one of the plague victims he'd learned about in Miss Cooper's history class. His eyes staggered along the kitchen worktop: egg basket, cereal tubs, fruit bowl...

'An apple would be great.'

Mrs Higgins washed one of the plump, organic apples, putting it on Danny's plate with a peeling knife and a napkin. Ignoring the niceties, Danny picked it up and wolfed into it in big juicy bites.

'Well,' said Mr Higgins, 'there's nothing wrong with your appetite. Watch you don't bite off a finger.'

What's up with me? wondered Danny. It felt like time slip, only worse. He often felt a bit rough when he came back from missions, but that was only like the skinny low-fat version of time slip compared to this. This was the extra-strong man-sized job.

He began slowly to switch his attention to the music that was playing in the kitchen. It was one of the *Interpreti Veneziani* recordings. The cool, crisp Baroque music began wafting through his head like a refreshing breeze. Mm, wonderful. And this apple was wonderful too, really delicious. Best apple ever, no question. He asked for another, and his parents watched fascinated as he demolished it. Danny crunched away, the fragrant juice somehow clearing his head till he felt better. No – much better.

He jumped to his feet, reaching for a third apple. 'For later?' he asked his mum. She nodded and smiled, puzzled. Boys! As a much livelier Danny zoomed out of the kitchen, Mr Higgins mumbled to his wife, 'It's probably something to do with his age.' No, thought Danny, it's probably something to do with time travel. For his mobile had begun to vibrate with the distinctive rhythm of a call from SHARP.

As he closed his bedroom door, Danny hit the black phoenix on his mobile to access the incoming message. The screen turned an intense blue, the image detaching itself and sliding upwards to hover soundlessly above the phone, a TV-sized, black-edged swirl of flowing colours.

Hi, Danny, it's Kaz - put your computer on so we can talk more easily.

He switched on his computer. The mobile screen shrank, slid back into place and went black. Simultaneously the computer display turned an intense swirling blue.

Cheers, Danny!

Hi Kaz, no problem.

Just wanted to let you know how pleased we are with how that mission went. My professor's really impressed. Good job, Danny! Sorry you got knocked off your bike by that bus thing. You okay?

Yeah, not a scratch.

Good! Just remember: your mobile's fitted with a protection shield that'll keep you safe. It activates automatically in the event of a threat from something like bullets or bombs.

Or charabancs?

Exactly! We all learnt a new word there – had no idea what a charabanc was.

Me neither.

Still, you were okay.

Yeah. Bit of a problem with time slip again, though. Worse than before.

Danny described briefly the symptoms he had suffered that morning.

Hmmm, sounds a bit worse than normal time slip. I'll ask our medics about it. For now, remember what we said before about getting over time slip. Focus really hard on your surroundings and it'll help stabilise you in the present.

Will do. Feeling better now anyway. So what about this World War 2 mission? I'm up for it!

Cool! I'll get back to you. But it's mad here just now – stuff going on.

Problems? STRAP?

Yeah. They're up to something. We think they're trying to infiltrate some of our agents and gain access to our systems. They're dangerous but we're onto them. Give us a few days to work on it, Danny. But I'll get back to you later about your time slip symptoms.

Cool!

The screen faded to Danny's usual configuration. He peered out at the rain washing over the neighbour's gnomes. Weird day. He'd felt lousy when he woke up, then ridiculously good over breakfast. He was more stable now, but what was all that about? Well, he couldn't hang around here all day. Round at Mark's there was, as Mark would say, some serious chillaxin' to be done! He grabbed his bike helmet and sprinted out.

It turned out to be good day. Hanging out at Mark's had been wicked. AJ had blasted everyone into oblivion at *Cosmic Time Warriors 3* like a true mind warrior, and it had been hilarious watching Griff getting zapped again and again. Danny lay staring at the bedroom ceiling in the glow of his bedside lamp. The house was silent, and outside the night rain hissed gently. Danny looked at the blue digital readout of his alarm clock, double dots marking the beat of the seconds. Better try to get some sleep but even as he looked away, one of the blue dots was still there in the centre of his vision. Danny blinked, as though somehow the dot had stuck itself onto his retina and he might shake it away. Still it hung there at the far end of his room, pulsating blue against the shadows.

As though from far away, Danny heard a shrill whine that seemed to get nearer. The blue light grew deeper, brighter. It wasn't a flash but a landing with merely a gentle pulse of violet light, a change in the texture of the air as it hardened into a solid body and the floor took its weight. There it was, in Danny's room, glowing with a soft blue radiance: the figure of a man.

The form took a silent step forward.

He was of medium height and athletically slender. He moved slowly, though his lithe physique looked capable of great speed. Danny couldn't guess his age. He was clearly not young, yet there were no lines around his black, almond-shaped eyes and his clear skin was stretched taut over sculpted cheekbones. His hair was night-black, cut with geometrical precision. His seamless one-piece garment was of a deep sapphire blue. Round his neck, on a smooth silver chain, hung a pendant shaped like a vertical eye, a double-pointed silver frame around a luminous blue stone whose glow shifted subtly from blue to violet and back. He looked, thought Danny, almost inhumanly perfect.

The man's thin lips arched into a cat's smile.

'Good evening, Danny Higgins. I believe you have been expecting me.'

'Have I?' Danny was astonished. 'No, I'm pretty sure I wasn't expecting this.'

'When we exchanged messages, I promised to meet with you. We discussed certain honours, a medal...'

Suddenly Danny understood. 'Professor Bucephalus Crumpshall?' he breathed.

The cat-like smile broadened. 'Please, call me 'Bertie': everyone does.' The voice was a softly lilting sing-song that oozed calm.

Danny nodded. He was still trying to stretch his mind round the fact that the ethereal, unworldly-looking being that stood before him was actually the stuffy-sounding Professor Bertie Crumpshall. He snapped himself out of it. But how was he ever going to explain this to his parents if they heard the sound of talking and came to investigate?

'Don't worry,' the professor murmured, 'we won't be interrupted'. He raised his hand which, Danny noticed, had six fingers and a thumb, that strange adaptation that Kaz had said so many future-dwellers had, and made a languid gesture towards Danny's alarm clock.

Danny glanced at the clock. The double dots that counted the seconds had stopped pulsing and now shone with a steady glow.

'I have stopped time around us. Though we shall feel time pass normally, for your family I shall have been and gone in an instant. But still, I must be brief.'

Danny listened, fascinated, to the purring voice.

'Danny Higgins, I am pleased to tell you that you are to be honoured with a further letter after your name as reward for your successful time travel missions. The suggestion that you should receive a medal is still being considered.'

Danny was not concerned about the medal, but the honour of the letter after his name – Yes, that was worth having!

'Cool. Thanks, Professor Crumpshall – that is, Bertie.'

The professor's strange pendant pulsed violet and mauve. 'You have earned it, Danny. I also have these for you.'

The professor gestured again to the bedside table, which just moments ago had held only the alarm clock and bedside lamp.

Though outwardly he kept his cool, Danny's mind reeled. On the table lay a sleek mobile phone and a small blue disc. Nobody had put them there: one second nothing, and the next they had just blipped into existence!

His pendant pulsing sapphire and purple, the professor murmured, 'These are yours, Danny: take them. They are the most advanced models our future technology can produce. The phone has,' he paused, 'certain special features. The blue disc is the latest disc recorder, like the ones you use on missions – but this one is permanent, wear-and-forget, just put it on and it will operate forever, invisible and undetectable.' He tilted his head like a hawk watching its prey. 'They are issued to only the very finest agents.'

Wow, thought Danny, these are cool, real elite stuff! And yet...

'Take them, Danny.' The professor's pendant shone a deep amethyst, a crimson star of light boiling at its core. His eyes held Danny's, unblinking as a cat's.

'Take them.' The pendant's depths throbbed like a ruby heartbeat.

Danny fought hard to focus. That serene voice was so compelling, almost hypnotic. There was something else, too – a musical hum right at the edge of hearing that intensified the sense of peace and calm. Was it coming from that weird pendant thing? There was something wrong here, something off balance. It didn't add up, and he wasn't comfortable with it! SHARP were subtle, but this was too much like a magic show. No, not SHARP's style!

The professor cut in. 'Put on the disc *now*. I shall remove your old mobile for secure disposal.'

Danny saw his chance, a slim one but worth taking.

'I'll need a bit of time to get the data off my old phone,' he said. 'You know – phone numbers, pictures, apps and stuff.'

'I can wait.' The professor's tone hardened, slivers of broken glass glinting in the velvet voice. The pendant flashed darker, the background hum intensifying.

Definitely something wrong here, thought Danny; SHARP are never pushy!

He pushed back.

'I'll do it first thing tomorrow.' Danny faked a huge yawn. 'It's the middle of the night, you know.'

For an instant Danny thought he had gone too far. The professor's pendant thrummed to a core of boiling black. His lips curved like someone who knew the correct order of muscle contractions to mimic a smile, but not its meaning. Then, suddenly, the tension

93

shattered. The feline features relaxed, the background hum receded, the pendant cleared to a limpid blue.

'As you wish,' the professor whispered. He gestured to the table. 'To launch the new phone's systems, key in your SHARP project number, 15798. We will know you have done so, and we will remove your old phone for disposal one hour later.' He paused, seeming to weigh Danny up, the hunting hawk again. 'You are strong-willed, Danny Higgins. I can see why you are an outstanding agent. I shall look forward to working with you.'

He took a pace backwards and, in a silent burst of pure lightning-blue energy, was gone.

CHAPTER 9

Destination: War

The morning rain fell from a sky that was the colours of an old bruise.

Oh great, thought Danny wryly, there's nothing nicer than a wet Friday morning in Nottinghamshire, when it's the last weekday of your half term holidays, your mates are off playing golf in the rain, and you've still got to decide on your Year 9 Options.

And then, of course, there was that strange visit in the night. There was no denying it; the weird Professor had left him feeling really uneasy; like he was being manipulated, bribed and pushed. SHARP's instructions had never made him feel like that before. But if Professor Crumpshall wasn't from SHARP, then who was he?

Two hours later, Danny leaned back in his computer chair and took another bite from his third apple of the day. What had started out as a pretty lousy morning, somehow had got better. He had cracked his option problem. The list was finalised, typed up and three copies printed out. It just remained to talk it over with his parents before Monday. He was just about to switch his computer off and go downstairs when the screen changed and a SHARP message started to come through.

Hi, Danny, it's Kaz. I see you're on your computer.

Hi Kaz. Yeah, think I've cracked my Year 9 options. Yaay!

Cool! I've got some news for you.

Fire away, mate.

Okay. First, the medics have come back to me about your time slip problem. I know you can handle it, but you were right to mention it. They reckon you've got chronoburn.

Chronoburn? What's that?

It's what happens when you get a build-up of time slip. One of the things that makes you such a great agent is that you're really sensitive to atomic resonance with the people whose places you occupy

when you travel. But it seems that some of this resonance sticks to your own atoms when you return to
your own time. It can build up over several trips and
become disruptive. It's a sort of atomic interference, a bit
like the members of a band playing together but all
playing different tunes: you get discord and you feel
off colour. Apparently if you don't treat chronoturn it
can turn into chroroburnout, which can make you really sick, Danny.

So what can we do about it?

Plenty! We'll adjust the transport settings on your future
missions, so you're still really sensitive when you're
there but you don't bring as much resonance back:
problem cured. But to clear up the effects for now, the
medics say you need to consume a source of an-
tioxidants, vitamin A, pectin and multiple amino acids.

Er, right! Where will I get that?

Apples! Seems they're full of that stuff. Eat one or two
and you'll feel better fast.

You're kidding – I've had an apple craving since

my last mission!

See? Your body's telling you what it needs. Another thing that makes you a top agent! Which reminds me – my professors have finished analysing your 1926 mission and say it's a total success.

Cool! Was it okay for me to give away that delivery boy's shilling? Was it a lot of money? Wouldn't like the kid to go short.

Perfectly okay. A shilling was worth the equivalent of about £2 in your time. We put the money back. Anyway, he had a pocket full of tips! Danny, you did so well we've approved the award of another letter from the word 'xrosmonaut' after your name to honour your successful missions, so you'll become Danny Higgins XrM.

Cool! But I sort of knew already.

What do you mean, knew? How?

The visit from Professor Bertie Crumpshall. He's a bit unusual for SHARP, isn't he? I mean all that glowing and creepy stuff!

Professor who?

Professor Bertie Crumpshall

Hang on a moment there, Danny. We don't have a Professor Crumpshall! This sounds really serious. Can you tell me everything about him? We need to know.

Swiftly, clearly, Danny described every detail of the strange visitation and the sleek new equipment he had been given. When he had finished the screen cleared, colours swirling. Four words materialised, flashing steadily:

›Stand by: security alert...

Long minutes passed, the words blinking maddeningly. Still no Kaz. What on earth?

Danny: sorry about that - I needed to speak to somebody senior here.

Kaz, what's going on? You okay?

Fine, Danny. Listen, we've a problem. About last night, as I said, there is no Professor Bertie Crumpshall at SHARP. He's not one of ours.

Then who was he? He was in my house! I felt like there was something wrong about him but I thought he was from SHARP so I didn't say anything.

Did he actually say he was from SHARP? Think hard.

Danny's mind raced through the night meeting and the messages he had received from this supposed professor two days ago, probing every detail.

No. Kaz, he never did. I guess I just assumed it. Stupid!

Danny, you're not stupid. You're an excellent agent. We think he – or it - used mind control techniques to put you off guard, a bit like hypnosis. The pendant, the weird hum, the voice, the cute nickname – all mind control. But you saw through it, Danny. Good work!

Thanks. But if he wasn't from SHARP, who was he?

A STRAP spymaster. Remember I said they're trying to spike our agents and infiltrate our systems? They've targeted you because you're a top agent. Once STRAP had you believing that Crumpshall was one of us he would have started sending you on missions we knew nothing about. We've analysed the mobile and recording disc Crumpshall gave you. The disc would have fed data back to STRAP all the time – your home life, contact with us, everything. The mobile would have copied all your SHARP messages straight back to STRAP, too, and sent you where they wanted you to go. And they'd have got your current mobile with its SHARP modifications – our secret technology. Their mobiles don't have automatic protection shields like ours – I bet they'd love to get their hands on those. Danny, you'd have been working for STRAP without knowing it! You've had a narrow escape, but we'll try to make sure they don't get near you again.

Whew! I'm beginning to feel as if I am in some war zone. Mind Control – I never thought I could be mixed up in something like that. It sounds strange, but now I feel more sure of SHARP than I did a few days ago. The fog's gone. I have to trust you Kaz. So what about that World War 2 mission?

Thank goodness you're still on side Danny! This one is a vital operation. I'll get back to you as soon as everything is set up properly and now we need to make sure we are protecting you from STRAP.

I'll be ready and waiting, Kaz.

The screen faded to Danny's usual screensaver. He glanced at his bedside table. The STRAP mobile and disc had vanished. So Crumpshall was a spy, eh? Sneaky lot, STRAP. Dangerous too. They'll have to do better than that to catch me.

For a while, life returned to the usual round of school, home and friends. Miss Cooper, Danny's history teacher, sent home a note saying how delighted she was with his new interest in twentieth century history, especially the twenties and forties. His parents were delighted with this new-found enthusiasm for their favourite subject, but Danny played it down as all being to do with a book he was writing – one they never got to see, that they suspected was probably just a jumble of notes on his computer. But their praise was encouraging, warm and genuine.

School done for the week, Danny headed for the park with Mark and Griff, carrying the tennis racquets that saw daylight for all of two weeks a year, around Wimbledon time. The park courts were damp and playing with three was tricky – AJ couldn't make it – but it was good fun.

It was that evening, as Danny was scrubbing off the school week under the shower, when the call came. The mobile skittered and danced on the glass shelf as the distinctive pulsing vibration came through. Wet-fingered, Danny answered. The screen slid and pirou-etted, expanding into place above the device, blue-tinged colours surging.

Hi, Danny. We've got the 'go' on the World War 2 mission! You've got two hours to accept it.

Cool – I'm good to go! Everyone'll be asleep here in an hour anyway.

Good man, Danny. I'll send through the mission brief now. Note there are special instructions this time – something we particularly need you to find out, so read the brief carefully.

Will do, Kaz. Any more news about STRAP's

spying activities? Did they get to any other agents?

We're still working on it as fast as we can, but there are a couple of the kids we've not been able to check up on yet. Crumpshall has certainly been busy and one thing is certain, he doesn't care whether or not they can bring back their agents as long as they get what they want.

Kaz , that is pretty dreadful – he's dangerous.

That reminds me, Danny. This is very important: the automatic protection shield that's fitted to your phone — try not to rely on it this trip. We've found that some agents' shields have been sabotaged by STRAP and could fail. Luckily nobody's been hurt. We'll have cracked the problem by the next time you travel, but just be extra-careful this time. We're pretty sure your shield will work, but this will be your most dangerous mission yet. You still good to go?

Always. Like someone once said to me, 'fortune favours the brave'!

Good luck, Danny! Here goes...

The screen cleared for a moment, darkening to purple, then...

‹Details of Current Travel Option›

‹Time Zone›
20th November 1940.

‹Place›
Buckinghamshire, England: just outside Bletchley.

‹Landing›
The lake at Bletchley Park, home of the Government Code and Cypher School, 'Station X'.

‹Instructions›
Change into the period clothes you will find.

‹Destination›
The main building at Bletchley Park that is known to everyone as the Mansion. You will know your contact when you see him.

‹Conditions›
Favourable. Weather benign. Wartime conditions – not

a battle zone. No disease risk.

‹Identity›

Donald Dempster, a Cambridge University undergrad-
uate student.
He is older than you, but excellent nutrition in your time
means you will be accepted as older than your true
age.

‹Equipment›

Mobile phone, travel bag. Mobile phone with beam of
light activated when t-o-r-c-h is keyed in (only use
sparingly). WARNING: the automatic protection shield
fitted to your phone may be prone to failure due to
sabotage. Try not to rely on it.

‹Special Instructions›

We need you to gather intelligence, if possible. Those
you meet on this mission may well be able to help
with the following:
STRAP project numbers (such as your 15798 project
number) might have hidden meanings, enabling the
agent to have great powers for evil once in the past.
We have learned that STRAP has an important new
agent, though we do not know his or her identity or

what they are doing for STRAP. All we know is that this new agent's project number is 19201. Knowing the meaning of that project number might help us to trace the agent and to limit the damage. Try to find the meaning of that project number. You have met two STRAP agents in previous adventures: Alex McLean, the boy you rescued from 1314, and Sarah Lacey, the girl you warned about working for STRAP. We now know that Alex's project number was 10810 and Sarah's was 10812. Try to find the meanings of those STRAP project numbers as well.

If you wish to travel, do as follows:
> Take off your clothes, except for underpants.
> Press the time/space travel bag close to your body so that it is attached.
> Press the green phoenix icon and key in 15798.

Good luck with this critical mission.

Danny read and reread the mission briefing until it was fixed in his mind, crisp and clear. His work with SHARP was becoming more complex and, by the look of it, more dangerous too. He didn't care. He was ready.

Midnight came and went. Slowly the household settled, lights went off and the hush of night descended. Only one light showed, the soft glow of the lamp by the bed of Danny Higgins XrM, time travelling agent of SHARP.

Searching the shelf over his bed, Danny found the small, flat, brown space/time travel bag tucked behind the elephant-shaped money box. As always, he hadn't seen it arrive. He felt the thrill of adrenalin course through his veins at the thought that he was about to step through time again. Wriggling into a pair of underpants, Danny pressed the travel bag to his tummy where it stuck fast like it was part of his skin. He ran over the mission brief that was etched into his memory. All crystal clear.

Danny picked up his mobile, pressed the green phoenix and when the keyboard appeared typed in 15798. He heard a faint high-pitched whine, far off, but coming nearer, louder, filling his head. Then...Nothing.

CHAPTER 10

Station X

It wasn't a jolt, the landing. Merely a surge of cool pressure as the warm carpet under Danny's bare feet changed to the damp chill of grassy earth and tendrils of frost-nipped grass curled upwards to brush his ankles. Brilliant sunshine flooded his closed eyes and the musty aroma of wet soil tickled his nostrils. There were the sounds of distant voices, of birdsong and of water lapping. The cold struck Danny like an icy hand and his eyes snapped open, focusing.

Greenery: a thick mat of rank grass underfoot, a dense tangle of tall shrubs all around. Through gaps in their branches he could see a broad patch of rushes fringing the edge of a lake. Danny took the recording disc from the travel bag and pressed it to his forehead, feeling the backing come away as the device dissolved into his skin. Reaching to slip the mobile into the travel bag, Danny noticed the screen. The number 15798 was still displayed across it. He hit 'clear': nothing happened. Again: still nothing. The number was stuck there. Weird, he thought. Hope that's not a fault – or sabotage...

Shivering, Danny spotted the clothes tucked under the shelter of a bush. He pulled out the bundle and dressed swiftly. There were long, cream-coloured woollen underwear, woollen socks, and a white cotton shirt. Over this went trousers and a jacket of fine, grey-green wool, like a modern lounge suit but a baggier fit. Completing the outfit were a dark tie, a voluminous woollen overcoat, and a college scarf. The clothes were a bit shapeless but warm and comfortable.

Danny laced on the shoes, smart brown brogues with a neat pattern of punched holes across the instep. Under the clothes Danny found a battered brown leather briefcase, and a greenish-brown canvas bag containing a black, rubber gas mask. He tucked the briefcase under his arm, slung the bag over his shoulder, and began to push through the shrubbery away from the lake.

Across the water the pointed gables of a large, old house loomed above the bushes. Was this the Mansion, his mission destination? He would have to find some way round the curve of the lake that separated him from it. He shouldered his way through the dense vegetation, which abruptly gave way to open space. A short grassy slope led up to a footpath. Stepping over the low kerb, he stopped to get his bearings.

To the right the path skirted the lake and curved out of sight. To the left it ran up to the house, which fronted a tree-dotted lawn. The path's farther edge was fringed with long, low wooden buildings stretching into the distance. They reminded Danny of Scout huts. Muddy paths ran between the buildings covered with duckboards to make a dry walkway. And the people: they were everywhere! Men and women in khaki army uniforms, in the blues of the Royal Air Force and the Royal Navy, and civilians of all ages marched, strode or bustled purposefully between the huts, or stood chattering in huddles. Everywhere was a buzz of activity. *Whatever's going on here, it's something big*, mused Danny.

He stepped back to allow a detachment of soldiers to march past, boots crunching, arms swinging, long brown rifles sloped over their shoulders, wicked steel bayonets glinting in the winter sun. A group of girls watched them, giggling, some seeming no older than kids in Danny's school year-group. As they hustled away, breath steaming in the chill air, a slim boy wriggled between them, pausing to glance at Danny from under floppy fair hair, then hurrying off on his errand.

Nobody else paid much attention. Danny set off towards the Mansion. He strode along a few paces behind two army officers, sunlight gleaming from their polished leather cross-belts and the silver-topped sticks tucked under their arms.

At first, in all the hubbub, Danny hardly noticed the shout; not even when it was repeated. Then from behind him came the clatter of heavy army boots running, slithering to a stop, followed by a bellowed challenge and the chilling *click-clack* of a rifle bolt.

'Oi, you! Halt or I'll fire!'

Danny froze, turned, and stared straight down the rifle barrel that was pointing right between his eyes. The briefcase dropped to the ground at his feet as Danny's hands flew up. The soldier with the rifle was screaming at him frantically. The rifle muzzle twitched alarmingly, the razor-sharp bayonet almost brushing Danny's nose. Danny clamped his eyes shut and waited for the bang.

'I say, what's all this fuss?'

The cool, upper-class drawl silenced the bawling soldier instantly. Danny opened one eye cautiously. Hearing the challenge, the two officers had turned back. The one who had spoken, a wiry man with a neatly clipped moustache, stepped forward.

'Put up your rifle, private.'

The soldier blinked, weapon still levelled.

'I said put up your rifle, private,' he drawled slowly, 'before you have someone's eye out.'

The officer reached out with his swagger stick and gently raised the rifle barrel skywards. It was enough to break the tension of the moment, but in an instant the soldier was roaring again.

'Sah, sah! I wuz on sentry duty sah an' I sez to my mate 'Arry I sez, 'Oo's that strange-lookin' beggar wot just come aht o' them shrubs? I mean this strange-lookin' beggar 'ere sah, an' 'Arry sez, *'E never come past this 'ere gate 'ouse so 'e never, let's nab the blighter!* so orff I goes arfter 'im but 'e _ust hignores me an' keeps goin'! 'E come from nowhere! I fink 'e's a spy, sah!'

The two officers exchanged glances.

'From nowhere? Hmm. Now look here, Private...'

'Binns, sah!' The private snapped to attention.

'Binns, you can't go waving a loaded rifle at whomever you please. This isn't Nazi Germany, you know.'

'Yessah! I mean nosah!'

The officer gazed quizzically at Binns, then at Danny.

'So, Binns, you'd have me believe that this...

this...' He wafted his swagger stick, grasping for the right word.

'Strange beggar, sah!'

'You're the strange beggar, Binns!' snapped the officer, losing patience. 'You're the strangest beggar there is round here, and that's saying something!'

The other officer stepped forward. 'Binns, you've been in trouble with me before for not paying attention whilst on guard duty.'

'But... but I wuz payin' attention, sah, beggin' yer pardon! But 'e never come past the gate 'ouse, sah!'

The officer fixed him with a steely-eye. 'So you mean to tell me, Binns, that this gentleman simply walked past you into a top secret military intelligence station? Or perhaps he just materialised out of thin air?' The two officers swapped wry looks.

Binns stood stony-faced.

'Report to my office in twenty minutes, Binns.'

'But... but sah...!'

'Twenty minutes, Binns. That'll be all. Dismiss.'

Deflated, Binns set off away towards the Mansion.

The two officers turned to Danny, who still stood with his hands aloft. One of them, a tall thin man with a neat moustache, tapped him on the chest with his swagger stick.

'You. Name and papers. State your business.' Impatiently, the officer plunged his hand inside Danny's jacket and tugged out a bundle of papers. 'Oh do put your hands down, there's a good chap,' he sighed. He unfolded the papers, scrutinised them thoroughly and handed them back.

'New boffin!' he exclaimed. 'Another one for Captain Ridley's Shooting Party!'

Danny's confusion was obvious.

'My little joke,' smiled the officer. 'When the first of you varsity types arrived here in '39, they put about a story that they were here for a shooting party with a Captain Ridley. To disguise the fact they were really all secret codebreaker chappies, you see. Well, now all the town knows something hush-hush goes on here – but what, eh? Mum's the word...' He winked and tapped his nose. 'Come on, you're to report to the Mansion.'

Danny retrieved his briefcase and chased the officers' rapid strides. Although it was hard to keep up with them, he managed to sneak a glance at the ID papers: Donald Dempster, mathematics student from King's College, Cambridge, not yet eighteen. Amazing! he thought: with SHARP's help, he looked old enough to pass for a university student!

As he neared the place the officers had called *the Mansion*, Danny got a better look at it. What a weird place – a real jumble! The house was an odd mishmash of architectural styles: gables and bay windows jostling for space with porches and a green, bell-shaped dome thing. Danny thought it must have been a large house before it became – what did the officer say? – a top secret military intelligence station. Its once-private grounds and gardens were now filling up with the wooden huts, some finished, some being built in a clamour of hammering and sawing.

Apart from the uniforms, there was little to suggest there was a war on. Bletchley Park bustled like a town high street, with that feeling that everyone was going somewhere important and had something urgent to do. The place swarmed like a beehive with purposeful people.

As Danny and the officers neared the Mansion, a group of four men emerged from its arched main entrance and stood together chatting. Two were in civilian clothes, baggy flannels and jackets, the others in the smart-as-paint uniforms of Royal Navy officers. One of the officers escorting Danny called out to this group, 'New boy for you here, Dilly!'

A tall, gangling man in his fifties turned to face them. He was one of the civilians. He had a mild expression that reminded Danny of a country vicar . His receding hairline, high forehead and the round spectacles that framed shrewd eyes, suggested extreme intelligence. The man's pursed lips broadened into a welcoming smile. He grasped Danny's right hand.

'Alfred Dillwyn Knox, known to all as Dilly, head of Cottage 3. Welcome to the zoo!'

'Dempster,' said Danny. 'Donald Dempster. Why, *the zoo*?'

'Because of all the strange beasties roaming around here,' quipped Dilly, waving a hand at the human traffic. The other men guffawed.

Danny glanced at the passers-by and grinned. They were certainly a mixed bunch! From girls barely in their teens to people who looked positively elderly; from smart military uniforms, to workmen in overalls, to scruffy eccentrics in ancient overcoats tied with string; it was a bizarre assortment.

'Come on,' said Dilly, 'we're breaking machines! Let's get you signed up and ready for Prof!' He strode off towards the big arched entrance, jacket flapping like the wings of a huge stork.

Bewildered, Danny scurried after him between

the carved stone griffins that guarded the arch and in through the double doors. Between Dilly's brisk manner and his helter-skelter brain, Danny hadn't a clue what was going on! He thought he'd better say so before things got even more confusing. Dilly stopped, clutching his forehead.

'Yes. Right. New boy and all that. Look, I'm going to get you processed. They'll put you on the books and set about finding you a billet.'

Danny looked blank.

'That means somewhere to live. And they'll sign you up to the Official Secrets Act, so we'll be able to discuss secret information. Essential if you're to work here. Then we'll see if your boss has turned up!' He took off again with speed.

'Boss?' called Danny, scooting after him. 'Isn't that you?'

Dilly stopped dead, Danny swerving like mad to avoid a collision. 'Good Lord, no! I'm just looking after you till Prof arrives. You'll be one of his Hut 8 mob!'

Danny was ushered into a room where several officers sat behind a long table that was spread with a grey army blanket. Danny's papers – identity card, letter of introduction from King's College, one from a government ministry telling him where to report and railway travel warrant – were inspected carefully. Then a major read out the Official Secrets Act 1911 which Danny signed, agreeing as a government employee that all information he learned would be kept strictly secret.

He was promptly whisked off to another room, where a bespectacled and grumpy army clerk took his details, telling him to come back later to find out where he would be living. 'If you're lucky it'll be at Woburn Abbey, the stately home,' the clerk whined. 'If you're unlucky it'll be a rat-hole with no electricity or water. Or some old dear reeking of lavender and widdle.' He gave a thin smile of grim satisfaction. 'But probably it'll be a pub – The Bull in Stony or The Green Man on Watling Street. Miles away. Borrow a bike. Next!'

Danny tottered out of the room. These secret intelligence officers didn't seem to have a very glamorous lifestyle!

'Tea!' exclaimed Dilly Knox, taking off down the corridor and swooping into a big room that had been converted into a kind of cafeteria. 'The main mess,' he said, taking in the whole place with a wafting hand. 'We work round the clock, so it's open all hours. Several like it around the Park. Hut 2's good, too. You'll learn.'

He nipped off and returned with two cups of orangey-brown, stewed tea. 'Hot, wet, vile!' he grimaced.

Danny sipped. Yup, vile! He eyed Dilly curiously. Is he my contact? What did SHARP mean by, *you will know your contact when you see him*?

Three men sauntered into the mess. Danny recognised them as the group who had been with Dilly Knox outside the main entrance. They collected cups of tea and joined Danny and Dilly.

'Gentlemen, Mr Dempster, new boy from King's for Prof's mob.' Then he addressed Danny. 'Dempster, this is Hugh Alexander, another King's man: Hut 6, though with his beady eye on a Hut 8 job, British chess champion 1938.' The gaunt, languid civilian nodded a greeting. 'The uniforms,' continued Dilly, 'are up from Naval Intelligence. We're working together closely. Commander Fleming and Lieutenant...'

'Smith,' supplied the commander, an imposing figure, tall and slim with an intense manner. 'My aide, Lieutenant John Smith.'

Danny exchanged a hand shake with all three men. He didn't believe that name for a second, but doubted that many people would ever challenge the haughty officer.

'Right, now Dempster I need to supply you with the background!' continued Dilly. 'Bletchley Park, Government Code and Cypher School. Top secret. Opened last year. Fighting the Nazis by breaking the secret codes their forces use to communicate. Knowledge is power. Know your enemy, what he's up to before he does it, and you can stay ahead of him. That's what we aim to do. Intercept coded messages, decode them, pass them to government for action. All without the Nazis even knowing we're here. Top secret.'

'Wow,' breathed Danny, 'you're spies! Real James Bond stuff!'

'Who?' asked the commander, raising one eyebrow.

Looking round the blank faces, Danny thought fast: maybe the films weren't that old. 'Just a friend,' he murmured, tapping the side of his nose. 'Hush-hush.'

'Quite,' said Dilly. 'Yes, spies. Though I'd rather call us cryptographers or cryptanalysts. Codebreakers. That's what you'll be too,' smiled Dilly. 'Vital work. Could win the war, save millions. One message at a time.' He paused to gulp the lousy tea.

'We work on Enigma, the enemy's most important secret code.' Dilly continued. 'Backbone of German military and intelligence communications.

Several different versions are used by their allies, too. Fiendishly complicated. And they're improving Enigma rapidly, making it far harder to break.'

'You've not broken the code yet?' probed Danny.

'Goodness, yes!' gushed Dilly. 'That was done by the Poles in '39. And we've done it many times since!'

Danny frowned, puzzled.

'But surely once you've cracked a code, that's it? You've got the key, so you can read everything written in it.'

'Ah, if only it were so simple,' murmured Dilly. 'Enigma is what we call a poly-alphabetic substitution cypher. That means that every letter isn't just encoded once: it's re-encoded over and over, every letter using a different key. Millions of permutations. And the keys are changed daily. So every day it's like a whole new code and we have to crack it afresh, taking several hours each time.'

'The enemy uses machines to encode and decode messages automatically,' said Hugh Alexander, the chess champion. 'Type in a message, out it comes encoded, and *vice versa*.'

'Enigma machines have several rotating alphabet discs and wiring plugs that can be set in various combinations,' explained Dilly. 'Their codebook tells them the setup combination for each day. That setup's the key to Enigma.'

'Pah! I say we send men in to pinch a machine and the codebook from the Nazis,' broke in Commander Fleming. 'Kill the guards, steal the goods. Ruthless. That'll sink them!'

"It wouldn't help.' Dilly protested. 'They'd just change the keys or upgrade the machines. No, we're going to have to break Enigma quickly, each version, every day, for the rest of the war.

Danny whistled quietly. So that's what Dilly had meant by *we're breaking machines* – they were breaking the complex code the machines created. Huge job!

'Trouble is, said Dilly 'what people outside, the war office and the ministry, don't understand is that this base is full of people who haven't slept for days, living on tea and sandwiches, catching a few minutes' doze at their desks. The work never ceases, a twenty-four hour operation at full pelt to break enemy codes and defend the nation.' He turned towards Danny. 'But we'd better get on Dempster, Prof will fill you in on everything else. Should be here any time.' He got up quickly and was off through the door, the others chasing along behind.

Outside, the air was cold and crisp.

'Prof's come up on the early train from London this morning,' said Dilly. 'Went up for an all-night meeting in Whitehall last night – ran the whole way there! Forty-odd miles. Brilliant long-distance runner. Brilliant man...'

He trailed off, staring hard down the long lake-side path.

'Ah, here's the very man now!'

A strange figure on a bicycle was pedalling hard along the path, bystanders hopping smartly out of his way. Every few pedal strokes he kicked the chain of his bike, to whose frame his leather briefcase was tied with frayed string. He wore a rumpled tweed jacket and faded, baggy flannel trousers. His brogue shoes were very scuffed, and he had forgotten his socks. Unless Danny was hallucinating, his shirt was actually a pyjama jacket. And oddest of all, he was wearing a gas mask!

The bicycle squealed to a halt. Prof fiddled with the straps on his gas mask.

'Mr Dempster,' said Dilly Knox, 'may I introduce the Prof. Head of Hut 8, Doctor Alan Turing.'

With a slurp of rubbery suction, Dr Turing pulled the gas mask from his face. Danny's mind whirled. My contact! Oh, yes, I know him alright! Bigger, older, but unmistakably the same person: he was the bicycle-riding schoolboy Danny had met in 1926! What had he mumbled back then? 'I'm touring...' Now Danny understood – he'd misheard. Not 'touring': *Turing*!

CHAPTER 11

The Mind Warrior

'I usually wear the gas mask in early June, when my hay fever is worst, because it filters out the pollen. But at the moment one of the local farmers is burning crop stubble which makes clouds of smoke and fumes, so if I wear the mask I don't have to breathe it all in!' Turing grinned.

Clever! thought Danny. Made perfect sense when you thought about it – but most people would be too bothered about how they looked! Yet Turing saw the world differently. Just two short weeks ago Danny had met this man, made friends and been there for him. But then it was 1926, and the man was an awkward schoolboy. For Danny, little more than fourteen days had passed, but for Turing it had been over fourteen years!

They rounded the end of the long wooden hut, hopping over a muddy puddle and onto the dry duckboards. Turing was a human dynamo, an impish bundle of energy. He whirled Danny on a lightning tour of Bletchley Park.

'Or Station X, as it's known,' he said. "'X' is the Roman numeral for ten, and this was the tenth site MI6 acquired for wartime operations.'

'And the whole place is one big codebreaking centre?'

'Aaaaah-W-Well-aaaaaah, no!'

That stammer had got worse.

'W-We're also a listening station. We intercept enemy communications. Radio signals, Morse messages, that sort of thing. Anything framed in Enigma code.'

'Which means breaking Enigma every day,' chipped in Danny.

'Precisely! Aaaah-ah-Imagine we intercept a N-Nazi navy message: U-boats – Nazi submarines - to patrol a particular section of the English Channel. We decode it, pass it to Naval Intelligence. Then up p-pops the U-boat to destroy some helpless m-merchant ship – and there's our Navy with a welcome committee ready to ruin their day! Lives saved, big help to the war effort. Well, that's the theory. Doesn't always work.'

High above and distant, their engines a hazy drone, a V-shaped formation of aircraft flew. Turing nodded up at them.

'Our fighters – Spitfires, probably. On their way to patrol for German bombers. The Nazis have been targeting cities for concentrated attacks: they call it a 'Blitz' – it means 'lightning'. At the moment it's Coventry's turn for a beating.' He let out a slow sigh. 'A few days ago Hut 3 – they handle Luftwaffe signals, the Nazi air force – they intercepted a signal about something big. Code-name 'Moonlight Sonata', a huge air raid being planned, all locations code-named to hide the targets. It was all passed on to government, who even had word the target would be the Midlands. But it all took so long. They took action, set up jammers to block the enemy guidance beams, put up fighters but when the Nazis came there were hundreds of them. Bombers. Aaah-About f-five hundred of Kesselring and Sperrle's finest, in three waves. Blew the heart out of Coventry, vast destruction, hundreds dead.' He shook his head. 'The ministry are blaming us for not giving enough warning. B-But with air raids there's only two or three hours' notice between getting a signal and the raid happening, and in that time we may have to re-break Enigma, work out what they're planning, pass it on... It's frantic. Pressure's enormous.'

Danny was staggered. 'But you're all working so hard!'

Danny watched Turing's face, deep-browed and snub-nosed. He watched the fighters trailing away eastwards towards – what? Victory? Death? The stained-glass-blue eyes, coolly observing the world from somewhere deep inside himself.

'Aaaah-H-Hard w-work's not enough!' exclaimed Turing. 'We can't go on like this: we must be clever, too!' He walked up to a door labelled Hut 1. The impish eyes lit up. 'Look at this!' He ushered Danny inside.

The room was long and low, with whitewashed walls, a bare floor and harsh light spilling from unshaded bulbs. In the middle of the space squatted two, huge machines. Each was well over two metres tall and almost as wide, great bronze-coloured boxes housing rows and rows of coloured drums in blue, black and silver, with wires and cable trailing everywhere. A team of young women scurried around, adjusting, checking, taking notes and observing.

Nothing could have prepared Danny for the heat, noise and smell of that room! The heat was stifling, the noise a deafening chatter of *clack-click-clacking*, the smell a suffocating stench of oil, grease and hot machinery. And it all came from those two great slab-like machines.

'What are they?' Danny yelled.

'Bombes!' bellowed Prof.

Bombs! Danny was horrified.

'No, *bombes*!' shouted Turing. 'They aaah-g-got that name because they sound like ticking bombs. But these aren't weapons, at least not like that. We fight with our minds at Bletchley! No: meet 'Victory' and 'Aggie'. My idea. They're code-breaking machines! They help do our thinking for us!'

'Thinking machines!' exclaimed Danny

'Aaaaah, Yes. You s-see, to break Enigma we have to run through thousands of possible solutions every time, one by one. A human codebreaker can only go so quickly because they need to stop for rest and f-f-food. G-Get a machine to do all that stuff – calculations, comparing coded messages against possible solutions, that sort of thing – and it speeds things up immensely! These things work faster than any human being and don't need rest. They'll do all the routine work and leave us free to do all the clever stuff!' Turing's face was glowing with boyish enthusiasm.

'Like electric brains!'

'Aaaah-aaaah-N-Nearly!' yelled Prof. 'Our brains are like onions – lots of layers of ability. Some of what they do can be done by a machine, if you break it down into steps. One d-day, we'll be able to create a machine that can do what *every* layer does, then it will be a genuine artificial brain! There'll be more like these, and they'll get better, stronger. These are just the first of their sort. For now, they're mostly good at comparisons and calculations: what we call 'computing'.'

'Computing? They're computers?!' Danny yelled in an excitement he could hardly contain.

'If the Nazis knew about these,' mused Prof, 'they'd bomb Bletchley night and day...'

'So why don't they?'

'Aaaah-B-Because they don't know! They must never know.' Turing's eyes held Danny's. 'The success of this war might depend on these machines and what comes after them. Maybe even the future of the world.'

They left the heat and din of the hut. Outside, the cool and quiet were soothing. In the blank, makeshift buildings, Station X fought its secret war. 'Hut 4, Naval Intelligence,' said Prof, waving an arm towards the long hut at the far side of the Mansion, the tower of St Mary's Church visible beyond the fence. 'Last stop on the tour!'

So far they had only gone into three of the huts. Hut 1 with the Turing bombe machines; Hut 3, Dilly Knox's outfit, Italian Enigma; and Hut 6, where Hugh

Alexander and the team slaved over German army and air force code.

'Won't be a minute,' Turing said, knocking at the door of Hut 4 and entering.

Inside was a maze of desks, many occupied by women. A fair-haired boy appeared from a back room carrying a cardboard box, saw the two visitors and promptly disappeared again. He seemed oddly familiar – who did he look like? Danny couldn't place him from that brief glimpse; maybe he just had one of those faces you think you know. A young girl came out of the same room carrying a pile of brown card files and smiled at Danny. Instantly dismissing the sort-of-familiar boy, Danny smiled back at the girl. Maybe he looked hot in forties gear!

Prof asked for Commander Fleming. No, he wasn't there. Then perhaps his aide was there? Yes, Lieutenant Smith could spare a minute. Prof went off and Danny was parked in a bare side room, empty but for a table and chair.

Left alone, Danny had time to think.

Danny had recognised Turing immediately. But what if he recognises me? Realises we met all those years ago? How would I explain why I've only aged a few days? But Turing had shown no signs of recognising him. Perhaps it was too far in the past.

That reminded him: his phone. When he'd landed his project number was stuck on the screen. Turning away from the door, he reached under his jacket and shirt into the time/space travel bag, pulling out the mobile. The number 15798 was still in place. No matter how much he tried it wouldn't budge.

'You alright there, dearie?'

Danny almost jumped out of his skin! He shoved the mobile into the open top of the travel bag and spun round. There in the door was one of the older Hut 4 ladies.

'Awww, sorry, ducks, did I give you a turn? Only I saw you in here all alone, like, and I thought I'd see if you were alright, not lost your way or anything.'

Danny smiled. 'I'm fine, thank you.'

'Good-oh, dearie,' smiled the grey-haired clerk, bustling away.

Phew, thought Danny, that was close! Never mind the Prof recognising me – what if anyone saw a mobile phone? What would they make of that! He didn't get much chance to think about it, for at that moment Prof returned and they set off again through the gathering dusk, towards Turing's own domain. Trudging along at the Prof's side, a thought echoed and nagged over and again: I didn't feel that travel bag snap shut...

Sitting in Prof's bare office in Hut 8, among heaps of papers, Danny picked up the slip of paper that Turing had slid across the desk.

'So,' said Prof, 'that's what it looks like: the Enigma code.'

DTHY HYSR CGNH DEJL AVZO SHUN

WLKN OPRT KIDT VHWL APUT DRTW

'Naval Enigma, to be precise. Always the same, written in groups of four letters. Could mean anything.'

Danny slid the paper back to him. It might as well have been written in Martian. He said so.

'Aaaah-Y-You'll c-catch on s-soon enough. I feel certain that secret work will suit you.'

Danny's eyes shot up from the paper. What did Prof mean by that? Had he recognised him?

'Can you know a secret and never tell? Ever, ever?' Prof murmured. 'Not even to those you trust most in the whole world? Can you do a thing and never breathe a word to a living soul till the day you die?' Turing smiled, breaking the tension. 'That's the secret world you've joined.'

For a moment Danny was speechless.

'Do give the fellow a chance, Prof! He's fresh off the Brain Train from Cambridge!' Dilly Knox stood in the doorway, beaming. He wandered in and pulled up a chair.

'Forgive Prof, Dempster, but he does love playing spies! Unless you've forgotten, Prof, I'm here for our meeting.'

One of the hut staff came in carrying a tray with a coffee pot and cups. Turing walked over to the radiator and began fiddling with a small padlock that closed a long loop of chain. Prof's coffee mug was chained to the radiator!

'W-Well,' said Prof, 'it stops anyone from walking off with it!'

'Merely one of Prof's many little eccentricities!' exclaimed Dilly.

'Aaaah-aaaah I-I-I'm not eccentric!'

'Pardon me, old chap,' observed Dilly, 'but even in a zoo like Bletchley you could take the prize for eccentricity. You noticed, Dempster, that when Prof arrived he kept kicking his bike chain? Prof, tell him why.'

'P-perfectly simple! The chain's f-faulty. Every fourteen pedal rotations it comes off. If I kick it, it stays on. What else should I do, hmm?'

'See? And then there's the Prof's lost treasure.'

'Aaah-D-Dilly, must you?'

'I must. This, Dempster, is the fellow who decided to play safe, just in case the war was to go badly. So he went around buying up silver and got it all melted down into two huge bars, worth – how much, Prof?'

'Aaaah-about £250,' mumbled Turing.

'Which,' said Dilly, 'is about half the current price of a decent house. Which bars he took into the woods near where he lodges, and buried.'

'For safety!' protested Turing.

'Indeed,' said Dilly. 'Only what have you done with them, Prof? Do tell.'

'Lost them,' grinned Turing. 'They'll turn up.'

'See?' said Dilly, loving it. 'Eccentric hardly covers it. Can't remember where he buried his life savings!'

Turing grinned. All the teasing just bounced off him.

'Prof uses his brain for thinking, not for remembering, I think,' said Danny.

'Of course, you're right,' agreed Dilly.

Midnight.

For hours Danny had sat at a paper-strewn desk copying messages for Prof. Time was getting on. Still he had not fulfilled SHARP's special instructions: to find the meaning of the STRAP project numbers and whether they were encoded with secret meaning. All evening Danny had worked, waiting for a chance to catch Turing on his own, but all evening he and Dilly had flitted about, in and out, never stopping, working tirelessly.

The sound of the door slamming jolted Danny wide-eyed. Dr Turing stood in the doorway, a brown envelope stamped 'TOP SECRET' under his arm. For a few moments he stood, watching Danny quizzically.

'C-Coventry's in for it again tonight. Hundreds of bombers went over earlier.'

Danny had heard the engines and thought nothing of it. What a world, where thousands of tons of explosive death could be carried by without a second thought.

'Y-You get off for the night. Be here bright and

early tomorrow.'

It's now or never! thought Danny.

'Prof, could I ask you about something? It's about codes.'

Turing nodded enthusiastically.

Danny took a sheet of paper from the desk and jotted down the STRAP project numbers: 19201, 10810 and 10812.

'Could these numbers be code for something?'

The codebreaker considered them carefully.

'P-Possibly. Do you have any more examples for me to go on?'

Danny thought hard. The only other project number examples he had were...

'These,' he said, writing down his own project number, 15798, and the next in the series, 15799. There must be a 15799 – SHARP once told him they'd re-cruited other agents after him.

Turing's eyes flashed wide as he read the first number, and for a long moment his gaze held Danny's. What was the matter with him? What was he seeing in those numbers?

'Where did you get this?' He tapped the paper, pointing to Danny's own project number.

Danny shook his head. 'I can't tell you that.

Sorry. It's top secret. Like you said, Prof, that's the secret world I've joined.'

'Hmm.' Prof scratched his head, frowning. He scribbled with his pencil for a few moments, then smiled.

'Aaaah-I'd say four of these five numbers are certainly coded.' He put crosses next to the STRAP numbers 10812 and 19201 and, astonishingly, the two SHARP numbers, 15798 and 15799.

'Th-They're what we'd c-call numerical transposition codes. Sounds hard but actually quite simple. You replace letters with numbers. Watch.'

Turing wrote out the alphabet. Beneath each letter he wrote corresponding numbers, first going up from 1, then counting back from 26.

A	B	C	D	E	F	G	H	I	J	K	L	M
1	2	3	4	5	6	7	8	9	10	11	12	13
26	25	24	23	22	21	20	19	18	17	16	15	14

N	O	P	Q	R	S	T	U	V	W	X	Y	Z
14	15	16	17	18	19	20	21	22	23	24	25	26
13	12	11	10	9	8	7	6	5	4	3	2	1

'The numbers you've given me use two slightly different keys. For 15798 and 15799, the rule is 'read off the letter; count backwards for the last letter'. For 10812 and 19201 the rule is 'read off the letter; zeros aren't letters'. Here, try it.'

Danny read the numbers off, noting the results.

'So 15798 gives the word AEGIS, and 15799 gives the word AEGIR!' said Danny.

'Correct.'

'And 10812 gives AHAB!'

Turing nodded.

Different keys: it would make sense that STRAP's code would be different from SHARP's.

'But what do they mean?' puzzled Danny.

'I might be able to help there,' said a voice. Danny looked up. Dilly Knox had slipped in unheard. 'It looks like the people who designed those code names were using ancient imagery. Before I became an intelligence officer I was a Classics scholar at Cambridge. Picked up all sorts – Biblical stuff, world mythology. The Aegis was a shield of extraordinary power that belonged to the Greek gods; also the bag that contained it, a store of great secrets. Aegir was the ancient Viking sea god, a powerful ally but a mighty destroyer.'

Power? Secrets? Is that what the two SHARP project numbers signified?! Danny's mind reeled. But what of the STRAP numbers?

'And this one – Ahab?'

Dilly frowned. 'Ancient Hebrew. An ancient king. Powerful but evil.'

Evil?! That was Sarah Lacey's project number!

'But this one,' mused Dilly, '10810 – it's meaningless. Could just be a smokescreen.'

'What about this one?' Danny pointed to 19201, the project number of the new, unknown STRAP agent.

Prof scratched his head. 'Hmm.' His eyes lit up. 'Ah! AITA!'

'Aita?'

'Yes, Aita! 1 – 9 – 20 – 1.'

'But I thought zeros weren't letters.'

'N-No - but don't you see? There are two letters for which the zero *must* be included: J, the tenth letter, and T, the twentieth.'

'Extraordinary,' murmured Dilly. 'Aita!' He glanced from Danny to Prof and back again. 'Ancient Etruscan. More ancient imagery. Aita was lord of the dark realms under the earth. The name means 'the invisible' or 'the unseen one'.'

For a few moments the room was silent.

'I won't ask again where you got these codes,' murmured Prof. 'But whatever they are, wherever you got them, I hope for your sake that you know what you're getting yourself into.'

The night was clear and cold, the half-moon bright as Danny left Hut 8.

Time to get out of here! He made his way along the lakeside path, heading for the bushes. Automatically his hand went to his stomach, feeling for the mobile phone in the travel bag under his clothing. He stopped. He felt again, pushing his hand inside his shirt. In an instant he was searching frantically. The bag was empty!

Danny's hands flew though his clothing checking pockets, linings, everywhere. It was nowhere! The precious mobile phone was gone, and with it his only means of returning home. He ran back towards Hut 8 checking the ground: nothing. He scrambled towards the door of Hut 8, nearly colliding with a boy who rushed out, head down, and hurried away. Where could he even begin to look? He'd been all over Station X today! The mobile could have fallen into the mud, or be under a desk in one of the huts, or? The huts:

Danny concentrated hard on that thought, fighting down the blast of adrenalin that made his lips and fingertips tingle and burn.

High above and distant, Danny could hear the intruding drone of a lone aircraft. What if the mobile had been found, if they thought it was some spying device, that he was a spy?

Focus: think...

Danny fixed his mind on the far sound of the aircraft engine, shutting out all else, slowing his quick breathing. The engine noise seemed to be growing louder, nearer, as he forced himself to concentrate.

Where did I see it last? Think... think...

Hut 4! There, when he was alone and checking the display, when the kindly clerk had surprised him. When he'd shoved the mobile back into the travel bag but didn't feel it snap shut...

It must have fallen out there!

Danny began to run, blood pounding in his ears, shoes crunching on the path then swooshing through the grassy lawn before the Mansion, the cold moonlight reflected from the nearby lake like a great bright eye.

Far away the night sky was split by the blue-white beam of a searchlight, sweeping the sky for the lone aircraft whose drone Danny could hear growing ever closer. He pushed on, rounding the broad front of the Mansion, heart hammering. Beyond in the gloom lay Hut 4, the loom of St Mary's Church beyond it.

The aircraft was close now, loud.

Danny looked up. Still the distant searchlight vainly swept the night sky for the plane – but there it was, picked out clearly in the moonlight sweeping high above the church. Danny could see the spectral grey expanse of its wings, the stark black crosses of the German Air Force. Like a great bird of prey it was circling, prowling.

Danny flattened himself against the wall of Hut 4, struggling to melt into the shadows. How could he get inside to look for his mobile without attracting attention? No time to think: he stepped from the shadows and reached for the door handle.

He recoiled suddenly as the door flew open, but not in time to avoid the figure that hurtled out and ran straight into him.

Danny?!'

Danny's mind spun wildly.

'AJ?!'

Pulling him into the shadows, Danny hissed, 'AJ,

what the hell are you doing here?'

'I could ask you the same!'

'Don't mess with me, AJ! I mean it.'

AJ peered at him from behind his floppy fringe.

'Are you working for SHARP?' No reply. 'Don't tell me you're working for STRAP!' Danny's brain teemed and swam with a million questions.

'How many missions have you done for them? How long have you been here?'

'I thought I was too young for this mission, but there are kids working here who are only just thirteen! I'm supposed to be the son of the man who runs one of the recreation huts – his whole family lives here. Then earlier today I saw you here...'

Suddenly, it all clicked into place in Danny's mind.

'You – you got here before me! The boy on the path when I first got here, then in Hut 4, then just now at Hut 8. It was all you!'

AJ's eyes met Danny's.

'Project 19201: it's you! The new agent, the 'hidden one'!'

'I'm just supposed to run errands round the place to help out, that's all. All STRAP want to do is watch what goes on here. I swear!'

Yeah, right, thought Danny. And they'll use that information for who-knows-what evil.

'Danny, there's something else.'

AJ held out a large, plain brown envelope with something bulky inside. The words 'TOP SECRET' were stamped across the front. Danny took it.

'I don't understand.'

'Danny – it's your mobile.'

'What?!'

'They sent me on an errand to Hut 8 a couple of hours ago, and I accidentally walked into Dr Turing's office. And there he was with your mobile in his hand! He must have found it somewhere, so I went back to get it. I thought STRAP might want it or something – your phones have automatic protection shields, ours don't. When I picked up the envelope I could tell there was something heavy inside, so your mobile must be...'

'AJ, you sneaked into Prof's office and stole it?'

'It was just lying in his office!'

'His *private* office! In a secret intelligence base! Marked 'top secret'! If they'd caught you they'd have arrested you for spying! And AJ - how was I supposed to get home without my mobile?'

He was a brave kid, Danny would give him that.

AJ stood up to him, started telling him why a time-travelling mobile phone couldn't just be left lying around in 1940. But Danny wasn't listening.

His eyes grew wide. Over AJ's shoulder, turning in on its final run, he could see the German bomber. With the church, the Mansion, the whole of Station X in its sights, it was coming straight for them.

As though in slow motion, Danny saw the aircraft swoop lower, moonlight glinting wickedly from its bullet-like plexiglass nose and swirling in its twin propellers. The long bomb bay doors swung open slowly.

Run! Yet even as the thought formed Danny knew it would be useless. They'd never outrun a falling bomb! Then the idea hit him.

'AJ, your mobile! Hit the escape! Key in your project number and hit the red button!'

The device was already in AJ's hand, his fingers fumbling the digits 1-9-2-0-1.

Danny flung a glance at the roaring bomber. From its wide belly he saw an object fall, heard a shrill, rising whistle, then...

BOOM!

The explosion tore the night with an ear-splitting roar as the first bomb hit somewhere beyond the church.

'AJ, go!'

'No! I won't leave you!'

'Just GO!'

The air was filled with a wild howl as the second bomb screamed earthwards.

'NO! What about you?!'

AJ's eyes were fastened on the approaching plane...

BOOOMMM!!

Danny felt rather than heard the second explosion, much nearer, right by the church and barely a hundred metres away. The flash was blinding, searing, a domed blast wave splintering the air and flinging a deadly hail of earth and stones and shattered tree branches screaming overhead. The stench of high explosive burned in Danny's nostrils and he knew, just knew that the next bomb would be right on top of them.

Danny wrapped his hand around AJ's and squeezed. It was a gentle pressure – but enough to push his finger down onto his mobile's red button. Danny let go. In a silent pulse of blue-white energy AJ was gone.

Danny tore at the brown envelope with frantic

fingers, scrabbling inside for his mobile. Above, almost on him now, the roar of the plane was mind-numbing. He ripped the mobile from the envelope.

No time to dial. No time. Time slowed to a crawl as Danny saw the third bomb tumble from the bomber's belly.

No time... no time...

He hit the red phoeniz.

His ears and mind were filled with the shrill shriek of the falling bomb, high-pitched, coming nearer, louder, filling his head. Then...Nothing.

CHAPTER 12

Across Space And Time

Silence. Darkness. Slowly, Danny opened his eyes.

Home.

From one hand dangled his mobile, from the other the torn brown envelope. There was still the acrid stink of high explosive in his nostrils. The mobile display flashed 15798, then slowly faded to black.

Danny shed his forties clothes, rolled them in the coat and stuffed them under his bed. He pushed the brown envelope behind the elephant-shaped money box. Numb, he flopped down onto his bed. He was asleep before the chill of the November night had faded from his skin.

At the first bleep of his alarm clock Danny was up and out of bed. It was only when he was in the shower, letting the stinging jets of water pummel him awake, that he realised. It's Saturday: no school, dopey!

Danny checked his mobile display: Saturday 23rd June 2012. He rubbed himself dry with the roughest towel he could find and headed for the kitchen.

It was a wide-awake Danny who, three minutes later, wandered into the living room with a steaming mug of tea in one hand and a half-eaten apple in the other.

Mr Higgins had his nose buried in the morning paper, while Jenny was curled up in a pink-slippered cat-like ball on the sofa, watching the early morning TV news.

'Morning, old man,' said Mr Higgins. 'Bit early for you for a Saturday, isn't it? Hmm?' He looked up from his paper. 'Danny?'

Danny was standing, apple poised mid-bite, staring at the television. Staring at the face that filled the screen, which was startlingly familiar...

'Dr Alan Turing,' said Mr Higgins, looking over the top of his paper.

'Yes – I know!' breathed Danny. I was with him only a few hours ago! he thought. In the night. In 1940...

'You alright, old man?'

'Mmm. Yeah, I'm fine thanks, dad.' But why would the morning news be showing... ?

'It's Turing's anniversary,' observed Danny's dad. 'He was born exactly one hundred years ago today.'

'Is he still alive?!'

'Goodness, no – he died a long time ago.'

In the bombing? wondered Danny. And Dilly, Hugh Alexander, Fleming, all the codebreakers and the boffins and... ?

The television screen switched to a weather map, snapping Danny back.

'Sorry, dad, what was that?'

'I said it's all in here, old man,' said his dad, rustling his newspaper. 'Big spread about him. Fascinating man, immensely clever. Before World War 2 he was a mathematician at Cambridge, then became a secret codebreaker when war broke out.'

'I know,' murmured Danny.

'Really?' His dad looked pleased. 'Then you'll be interested in this. Seems that during the war Turing worked on machines to break the enemy Enigma code. That work helped us to win the war, perhaps saved millions of lives. Winston Churchill, Britain's wartime leader, said Turing made the single biggest contribution to Allied victory in the war against Nazi Germany: imagine - that's a huge thing!'

Danny listened, fascinated. His dad warmed to his theme.

'Doesn't end there, old man. His codebreaking machines were developed into more powerful devices that were the ancestors of our modern computers. Then after the war Turing actually worked on designs for the first electronic computers, up at Manchester University.'

'So he survived the war!' Danny's relief was obvious.

'Yes, old man, he did,' said dad, surprised by his son's sudden emotion. 'In fact the work he did on computers was so important that he's sometimes called the Father of Computer Science. Seems he was a fantastic athlete too – a top marathon runner: he might have competed at the 1948 Olympics but for a knee injury.' Dad shook his head in admiration. 'Amazing chap. And he had Asperger's Syndrome, you know. Maybe one of the most important people of the last century. A very modest man, too. Maybe that's why he never got the honour he deserved.' He smiled. 'Glad you know about him, though.'

'What happened to him?' Danny was thinking of the quirky boy on the bicycle who did make it to school. Who did so much more.

'He died in...' Mr Higgins checked the newspaper article. '... in 1954. June. Only forty-two. No age, really.'

'How?'

'Well, old man, it's not all that straightforward.' He folded the newspaper and steepled his fingers.

'The generally accepted idea is that he killed himself. He's supposed to have poisoned an apple with cyanide, then eaten it.'

'What?! Why?' Danny couldn't imagine that swift, brilliant mind doing such a thing. What could push someone to that?

'Well, it was to do with his personal life. Dr Turing preferred... well, certain relationships that today we wouldn't find unusual. The fact was, Danny, he was gay. But he lived in less open-minded times. Then those relationships were against the law, and he got into trouble for it. The idea is that he became depressed and decided to end it all.' Dad paused, thinking. 'But I don't believe it.'

'No?'

'No, old man. You see, too often people just repeat what they've heard: they don't think for themselves, don't examine the evidence. But I have, and I think his death was an accident.'

Danny was fascinated. 'Why?'

'When Turing died there was an inquiry. They

decided he'd killed himself, but I think they were mistaken. Records of all the evidence – medical reports, police reports, witness statements and so on – were kept, and you can read them on the Turing Digital Archive website that's run by King's College, Cambridge. It seems that just before he died Turing had been working with chemicals at his house in Cheshire, gold-plating some teaspoons as a present for his mother. He often did little projects like that, and he'd turned one of his bedrooms into a laboratory. And what d'you think they use in the gold-plating process? Cyanide! Whole house reeked of it. He'd left the plating apparatus running while he was asleep, so he was probably breathing in the fumes. And nobody ever tested the apple they found by his bed, the one that he supposedly laced with poison, so that's no more than a theory. No, I don't think he killed himself: I think he was just careless with poisonous chemicals. Careless and absent-minded.'

Absent-minded? thought Danny. The act of a man who could bury two big silver bars, then just forget where he put them...

Dad handed Danny his folded newspaper. 'Here, old man. Have a read. And have a look online – make up your own mind.'

'Cheers, dad,' said Danny. 'I will.'

He headed for his room.

As he flipped on his computer, the display immediately turned an intense swirling blue and the familiar stark text appeared.

Hi, Danny! Excellent mission!

Thanks, Kaz. Not an easy one.

True: but you did a fantastic job.

Bit of a close thing at the end, though! That bomb...

The automatic protection shield on your mobile was working fine. You were never in any danger. But AJ was: STRAP mobiles aren't fitted with shields – just another example of how they expose their agents to danger. Danny, you saved AJ's life!

He's a decent guy – he didn't want to leave me there. But that project code of his - Aita, ruler of the dark realms, the hidden one. Sounds evil! Kaz, what has he got himself into?

Hidden and evil just about cescribes STRAP, Danny. We'll send someone to talk to AJ, try to find out more about Project AITA. We'll monitor Station X, too, in case STRAP send back one of their killers to cause chaos.If they do, we'll deal with it.

Danny, we don't think AJ understood who he was dealing with, how evil STRAP really are.

The SHARP numbers were code too! AEGIS and AEGIR!

A shield of extraordinary power, a store of great secrets? A powerful ally and a mighty cestroyer? That's what we do Danny, who we are: we're fighting STRAP. Fighting for humarity.

Kaz, that German bomber. Was anyone hurt?

We think it was a random attack – a plane on its way home, looking for somewhere to dump unused bombs. They didn't know what they were bombing. But everyone was fine! Hut 4 got blown off its foundations, but that's all. No casualties. Three other bombs hit Station X, but none of them exploded. Weird.

You're kidding! Another bit of SHARP wizardry?

Not us, Danny: pure luck! Maybe the Universe was looking after Alan Turing. One last thing: we were a bit concerned about sending you back to 1940 because you'd met Turing as a boy. Always a risk he'd recognise you and give you away. Danny, the feed from your recording disc was fuzzy – that's often caused by atomic interference when someone recognises our agent. Could have been Turing – but it might have come from AJ, too.

Anyway, gotta dash: good work, Danny Higgins XrM!

The screen swirled blue, then faded to black.

Danny gazed out of the window at the neighbour's gnomes, enjoying an hour's sun for once. The sun filtered into the space under his bed. It was clear, the bundle of clothes gone. He thought about Bletchley. What had happened to his mobile while it was lost? And why did Turing react so strongly when Danny had written down his project number – was it because Turing had just seen it flashing across the screen of this strange device? What did he learn from the mobile – and what would have become of it, sealed in that top secret envelope?

So many questions. Now I'll never know. He thought about the boy who became the Prof, born a century ago today; the boy who loved apples, who promised to pay back a borrowed shilling; the man who fought a war with his mind. Had he really recognised Danny?

The sun picked out the elephant-shaped money box on the shelf, the empty brown envelope stamped 'TOP SECRET' tucked behind it. Best not leave that lying around, he thought, pulling out the envelope. As he did so, a small white object dropped out onto his bed. He picked it up.

It was a note, wrapped tightly around something flat and hard. He opened the paper carefully and read.

Dear D,

I think this is yours.

Regards,

Alan

Danny held up the little object to the bright morning sunlight. There was a postscript to the note.

P.S.: Keep the change

The light glinted from the newly-minted surface of a bright silver 1940 shilling. Across time and space, Alan Turing had paid him back.

Can you know a secret and never tell? Ever, ever?

Danny grinned.

'Happy birthday, Prof!'

Acknowledgements

My sincere thanks are due to the following people:

Judy, my ever-patient wife, without whom nothing would be possible;

Jane Schaffer of Seven Arches Publishing for her belief in this book and her editorial dexterity;

Amanda Purkiss for an introduction *sine qua non*;

Christopher MacCafferty and Kelvin Pak, true friends, for their unfailing faith and encouragement;

Abigail Maher and Dr John Smyth for their constant support and technical guidance;

Rachel Hassall, School Archivist of Sherborne School, for historical advice and for access to documents and photographs

And to Dr Alan Mathison Turing:
IEKYF ROMSI ADXUO KVKZC GUBJ

Collect the other exciting books in the Time Traveller Kids series and discover the history of famous sites in the United Kingdom

Danny's interest in history is zero, but when a mysterious boy, claiming to be from a future organisation called SHARP gets in contact with him on his mobile, Danny agrees to travel back to the Tudor period. Making friends in the long-forgotten past gets him seriously hooked on time travel, not to mention history!

Danny has become an experienced time traveller but this doesn't help him when SHARP's communication systems fail. It is the year 671, the Dark Ages and he is left stranded in the depths of winter when wolves roamed the English countryside and Danny cannot understand a word the strange people speak.

Incredibly musically gifted, Atlanta is entranced by the music of the far-into-the- future humankind. Is this what makes her agree to join the growing band of twenty first century kids who go back in time to gather information for the organisation called SHARP?

When Alex McLean is catapulted back to 1314 by a rival outfit to SHARP, his life is in serious danger. This organisation, called STRAP, do not care if he falls to his death when he joins the desperate band of Scots fighters who did the impossible and scaled the terrifying Rock on which Edinburgh Castle stands to this day.

Jo Kelly's parents, both Oxford Academics, are so busy fussing over her super bright brother, who is a chorister in the world famous Magdalen College choir, that they don't realize they are ignoring Jo. How envious they would be, if they knew that Jo is sent back in time to Oxford 1939 and that she actually meets the legendary C.S. Lewis and J.R. Tolkien.

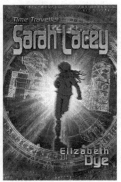

When ten-year-old Sarah accepts the challenge to travel back in time, she thought that she might meet Robin Hood. She had not bargained on joining a band of half-starved children toiling deep under ground in a south Yorkshire coalmine. She becomes a 'trapper' – a child who pulled a string to open a trap to let the trucks of coal hurtle onwards down the tunnel, that is until the mine started flooding. Sarah's life is in danger!

The Blog

If you've enjoyed this book, go to Danny's Blog for an exciting FREE read.
www.travellingthroughtimeispossible.wordpress.com/

Competitions And Activities

Seven Arches Publishing often runs competitions for you to enter with prizes of book tokens, that can be spent in any bookshop, for solving puzzles or for a good illustration. Why not go to
www.sevenarchespublishing.co.uk
and check out whether there is competition or activity on its way based on one or other of our books. We often include the winning entries of our competitions, or the writing, poems or pictures that you send us in the next print run of the title.

Contact Us

You are welcome to contact Seven Arches Publishing by:
Phone: 0161 4257642
Or
Email: admin@sevenarchespublishing.co.uk